How could he resist her?

'Eve—it's nearly midnight. You really ought not to be here now,' David muttered in a voice that did not seem to belong to him.

Her mouth invited his kiss, her moist pink lips parted softly for him. How could he not touch her? His thoughts were lost in the long, deep, all-absorbing kiss, which took away all caution. There was no past and no future, only the incredible present moment.

Dear Reader,

Welcome to Medical Romances! This month sees the innovation of an editor letter, which we hope you will find interesting and informative.

We welcome back Betty Beaty after a long absence from the list, and launch Margaret Holt with her first book, as well as offering Kathleen Farrell and Hazel Fisher— happy reading!

The Editor

Margaret Holt trained as a nurse and midwife in Surrey, and has practised midwifery for thirty-five years. She moved to Manchester when she married, and has two graduate daughters. Now widowed, she enjoys writing, reading, gardening, and supporting her church.

Margaret believes strongly in smooth and close co-operation between the obstetrician and the midwife for safe care of mothers and their babies. This is her first Medical Romance, which has won the New Writers Award of the Romantic Novelists' Association for 1992.

A PLACE
OF REFUGE

BY

MARGARET HOLT

MILLS & BOON LIMITED
ETON HOUSE   18–24 PARADISE ROAD
RICHMOND   SURREY   TW9 1SR

To my wonderful colleagues,
midwives and auxiliaries at TGH

*First published in Great Britain 1992
by Mills & Boon Limited*

© Margaret Holt 1992

*Australian copyright 1992
Philippine copyright 1992
This edition 1992*

ISBN 0 263 77660 3

*Set in 10 on 12 pt Linotron Plantin
03-9205-55230*

*Typeset in Great Britain by Centracet, Cambridge
Made and printed in Great Britain*

CHAPTER ONE

IT WAS Saturday evening, and the hands on the clock tower of Beltonshaw General Hospital pointed to ten o'clock. The outline of the solid grey building with its rows of lighted windows one above the other had almost the appearance of a great ship, a passenger liner riding the industrial and suburban landscape under a black February sky. Behind those windows the night staff were settling their patients, giving out the last drinks, checking sedatives and pain-relieving drugs, recording four-hourly temperatures, pulses and blood-pressures, examining dressings and adjusting intravenous drips. In one ward after another, the lights dimmed to a faint red glow.

Over in the maternity department at the rear of the hospital, the lights still blazed in the consultant delivery unit on the first floor, above the post-natal and special care baby unit. Two white-coated doctors were making their way up the stairs to CDU. One was Chris Roberts, a cheerful junior doctor, a houseman on the obstetric team. The other was a well-built, broad-shouldered man whose brooding dark eyes behind heavy horn-rimmed spectacles gave him a sombrely handsome appearance. His expression was guarded, even aloof, and glints of silver in his thick, dark-brown wavy hair made him look older than his thirty-three years.

'I hear that the night nursing officer on Maternity is quite a character,' he remarked in a deep voice that held a faint trace of a clipped South African accent.

'Rather! Miss O'Casey rules her staff with a rod of

iron, but she's a damned good midwife, and I've learned a lot from her,' admitted the younger man. 'She's away on a refresher course this week, though I think she's on tomorrow night. I suppose you know that the midwives have to clear off every five years or so to these talking-shops. There's an ice-cool blonde in charge tonight—her name's Eve, very suitably because she must be the original temptress reincarnated. Wow!'

His companion raised a quizzical black eyebrow but made no comment. They reached the top of the stairs and made their way along the main corridor connecting the ante-natal ward to the CDU with its two delivery rooms, two stage one rooms, maternity theatre and waiting-room. They headed to the central office, where a pretty, rather tired-looking young staff midwife sat at the desk talking to a plump nursing auxiliary.

'Hi, Annette, how's life? Is Sister West around?' asked Chris.

'Yes, I'll go and see if she's free,' replied Annette Gardner, obediently getting up.

'I say, Nancy, is there any chance of coffee?' suggested Chris with a wink at the auxiliary.

'I'll see what I can do,' she smiled, with a questioning look at the other man as she went out to the kitchen almost opposite the office.

'They're dying to know who you are, but I'd better wait until—ah, here she is!' exclaimed Chris as Sister Eve West entered the office.

'Good evening, gentlemen.' Her glance went at once to the newcomer, who gave a gasp of surprised admiration, though he quickly recollected himself. Eve West's stunning good looks and perfect figure always caused men's heads to turn wherever she went. Doctors, technicians, porters, ambulance men, even the husbands and boyfriends of her patients tended to look twice at the spectacular blonde midwife on night duty at Beltonshaw General. She was dressed in her navy uniform, her bright corn-coloured hair drawn softly back into a coil at the nape of her neck, and a crisp white cap adorned the crown of her head with no visible means of support. Wide grey-green eyes looked from one doctor to the other, and her coral lips parted expectantly as she too waited to be introduced.

'Eve, this is Dr David Rowan, who's come over from Johannesburg to take up his appointment as obstetric registrar on Mr Horsfield's team,' explained Chris, noting her immediate awareness of Rowan's reaction. She held out her hand with a demure smile of welcome, and David Rowan took it, giving a slight inclination of his head.

'I'm very pleased to meet you, Sister West.'

She lowered her eyes under sweeping blue-black lashes.

'Likewise, Dr Rowan. We weren't expecting to meet you until next week.'

'I was about to explain,' went on Chris. 'Mr Andreasson should be on call for this last weekend before he leaves, but he's got the most lethal cold—streaming like a tap, poor chap, with a sore throat and splitting head. When Mr Horsfield heard that Dr Rowan had arrived in Beltonshaw, he asked him if he'd care to start a few days early, without the usual trailing around with his predecessor. And that's why a mere junior doctor has been given the honour of introducing him to you!'

Eve nodded. 'I see. You're being thrown in at the deep end, Dr Rowan. I don't know how Manchester will compare with Johannesburg—certainly not weather-wise!—but you're fortunate to be working under Mr

Horsfield. He has to turn down a great many applications.'

'Yes, I hope to take my fellowship while I'm here,' he replied.

'You're going to be busy, then, working and studying.' She knew that the examinations for the fellowship of the Royal College of Obstetricians and Gynaecologists were notoriously difficult.

'That's right. I'm not here for the social life, Sister.'

'Indeed? I'd better get my hostess's duties over quickly, then,' she replied coolly while Chris Roberts grinned behind Rowan's back. Eve's poise and total self-confidence were a match for any disdainful know-all from South Africa, the junior doctor thought with satisfaction.

'This is Staff Nurse Annette Gardner, who has recently qualified as a midwife—and Nancy is our nursing auxil-iary on duty tonight,' Eve continued, and Rowan nodded to each of them in turn, accepting a mug of coffee from the tray that Nancy had brought in and set down on the desk.

'We also have Sister Doris Hicks on duty for the ante-natal ward. She's just seeing to a patient who's for induction of labour tomorrow. So much for the staff. You will, of course, want to know about the patients at present in labour. There are two, both primigravidae. One's a lady in her early thirties, very anxious to have a natural childbirth, but the pains proved to be stronger than she'd expected, and she now has an epidural anaes-thetic which Dr Grant commenced at nine-thirty p.m. She's much happier now, and so is her husband. The other is a schoolgirl, only just sixteen. Her parents are with her, and I intend to deliver her myself because of the circumstances. Apart from calling Staff Nurse Gardner to stand by at the time of the actual delivery—

we always have two midwives present—I don't want anybody else around.'

Dr Rowan nodded.

'As long as you call us at once if you run into any problems, Sister. Perhaps I ought to just say hello to the little girl, and maybe take a look at the other lady. I don't know whether you or Staff Nurse Gardner have got time to show me around the unit. I'd like to have a rough idea of the geography if I get called out tonight. I have a room in the medical residency, and I'm carrying Mr Andreasson's bleep.'

'Good.' Eve's enigmatic smile once again caught David Rowan off his guard. Never before had he encountered such an exquisitely lovely woman, he thought, bewildered by the suddenness of the attraction.

Chris Roberts broke in with a spice of devilment, 'By the way, Sister West belongs to a very fortunate paediatrician, Phil Cranstone, who's doing a course at Christie's at present——'

'I beg your pardon, Dr Roberts, but I don't belong to anybody. I'm my own property,' retorted Eve with a flush of annoyance.

Nobody noticed that at the mention of Philip Cranstone Annette left the office abruptly, her pale little face tense with resentment. Chris shook his head, but did not apologise: he had his own thoughts on the matter.

'Would you like to come and see Melanie Sayers now, then, Dr Rowan?' asked Eve. 'I'm about to do her half-hourly observations.'

Rowan followed her to Stage One Room B, where the young girl lay on the bed, her mother seated beside her.

'Hello again, Melanie dear,' whispered Eve in a completely different voice from the impersonal tone Rowan had heard in the office. 'All right, Mrs Sayers, don't get up. This is Dr David Rowan, who is on call tonight, just in case we need a doctor for any reason. No need to worry, you're doing fine.'

'Hello, Melanie. Good evening, Mrs Sayers,' smiled Rowan. The schoolgirl stared at them with frightened eyes as another wave of pain began to grip her contracting muscles.

'All right, chick, breathe your pain away, nice deep breaths in and out,' soothed Eve, gently wiping the girl's forehead with a moist facecloth.

'I can't, I *can't!*' cried Melanie, writhing in the bed and clutching at her mother's hand. Her father's face appeared round the door, but he hastily withdrew and resumed his pacing of the corridor, unable to watch the agony of his daughter, who should have been studying for her GCSE examinations in June.

'Easy now, Melanie, the pain's going off again now. Steady, dear,' said Eve softly. David Rowan felt sad for the Sayers family, and for the new arrival making the mysterious journey into the world, unplanned and unwanted.

'Is there anything she can have to ease the pain, Sister?' implored Mrs Sayers.

'Yes, my dear, but I shall have to do an internal examination first, to see how far Melanie has progressed,' replied Eve, looking towards Rowan, who withdrew, leaving her to perform the assessment, gently using her gloved right hand to probe into the vagina and feel the dilatation of the cervix.

'Well done! Five centimetres already,' she said reassuringly as she withdrew her hand. 'I'll bring you an injection that will help you to cope with the pain.'

Back in the office, she found that Dr Rowan had been confronted by chatty Sister Hicks, a widow in her fifties

who worked part-time. She had hurried over from Ante-
Natal as soon as she had heard from Nancy of the new
registrar's arrival.

'Ah, Doris—will you check this meptid and maxolon
for me?' requested Eve, unlocking the drug cupboard.
Together the sisters examined the two ampoules, and
signed their names in the controlled drugs book, with
Melanie's name and the date and time. Eve returned to
Stage One Room B where she gave the injection into
Melanie's bottom, so swiftly and expertly that the girl
felt only a brief stinging sensation. Within a few minutes
the pain-reliever and the anti-sickness drug began to take
effect, and Melanie drowsed between contractions,
though continuing to moan softly as they came and went.
Her father felt able to come in and sit with his daughter
for a while.

'I see that the baby's for adoption,' remarked Rowan
as he glanced at the case-notes.

'So it says *there*, Doctor,' replied Doris Hicks knowingly. 'But they'll decide to keep it as soon as they see it,
you mark my words!'

'But it would be so much better for the kid to go to a
childless couple, surely?' protested Rowan.

'That may be your opinion, Doctor, but the Sayers
family will have theirs, and nothing anybody says will
make any difference,' said the older midwife firmly.

Eve re-entered the office and wrote down her latest
observations in Melanie's case-notes.

'It's a situation where there's no cut-and-dried solution,' she said with a sigh, wishing that Sister Hicks
would not talk so much. Dealing with a terrified teenager
was not like talking to a mature woman who could listen
to explanations and instructions, and the parents were as
much in need of emotional support as their daughter.

Eve knew that she was going to need a lot of patience and a certain amount of firmness.

'How far on is the other lady?' asked Rowan.

'Mrs Blair was only three centimetres when I examined her just before the epidural. Dr Grant put up an intravenous drip, of course, and her blood-pressure's stable.'

'Good. I'll be off, then, Sister, and Dr Roberts can bleep me if you have any problems that he can't handle.'

'Or that *I* can't handle, Dr Rowan.'

He felt the direct gaze of the grey-green eyes that held a little gleam of amusement, and on an impulse he held out his hand.

'I do hope that we're going to have a good working relationship, Sister West,' he told her. 'I'd appreciate that.'

And for the first time since their meeting a warm and friendly smile transformed his rather saturnine features; Eve experienced a sense of warmth and security that was quite new to her, and hardly knew how to respond. She was used to exercising her power over men, but she felt instinctively that this one could cut right through her defences if she allowed him the opportunity.

Releasing her hand from his after the briefest touch of her fingers on his palm, she lowered her eyes and turned away.

'I'm sure we shall, Dr Rowan,' she murmured. 'But I hope I shan't have to disturb your sleep tonight.'

He regarded her retreating figure, her straight and slender back and perfect legs as she returned to Melanie Sayers's bedside. Eve West was not only a very beautiful woman, he decided—she was a temptress and a tease. And extremely fascinating. His dark eyes were thoughtful as he turned and went down the stairs.

Sister Hicks nodded towards Nancy.

'I may be wrong, but I think we've just witnessed love at first sight.'

'But she's engaged to Dr Cranstone,' objected Nancy.

'Not officially—and he's not here to keep an eye on her. Mark my words, I know Eve West. She can't live without a man, and unless Philip Cranstone——'

'Sssh!' hissed the auxiliary as Annette came into the office, and Sister Hicks suddenly became very busy recording the four-hourly blood-pressures in the case-notes of her patients. Annette pretended that she had not heard their exchange, but bitterness against Eve raged in her heart. It had been bad enough to see her beloved Phil so easily bewitched by this shallow-hearted woman: had she now got to watch him being betrayed as soon as his back was turned?

At midnight Mrs Sayers frantically rang the call-bell in Stage One Room B.

'Please come to Melanie, Sister! Something's happen-ing! Quick!' she cried in panic. Eve hurried in immediately.

'I want to push down, Mummy, and I can't stop myself!' Melanie gasped, her voice full of fear.

'Ssh, ssh, Melanie, there's no need to panic—nor you, my dear,' Eve said kindly but firmly. 'You'll have to do as I tell you, and everything will be fine—you'll see.'

She quickly ascertained that stage two of labour had commenced: the cervix was fully dilated. Melanie would need all the encouragement and support that Eve could give her, to enable her to stay controlled and push her baby through the birth canal.

Having already decided to deliver Melanie in the stage one room rather than the more clinical atmosphere of the delivery room, Eve swiftly wheeled in a delivery trolley and a heated cot, checking that all was ready for the care of the young mother and her newborn baby. All three of them found the next twenty-five minutes very hard work.

'Come on, Melanie love,' urged Eve towards the end of stage two. 'Give me another little push, go on, and another—that's right, keep it up, keep going—there's a good girl. Well done! Stop pushing now, and pant in and out like a puppy-dog, that's the girl, pant in and out, in and out—have you got the syntometrine ready, Annette? Yes, please—give it now.'

'Oh, Melanie, the baby's head's born!' cried Mrs Sayers. 'Oh, bless it, my little grandchild. . .'

At twelve thirty-five a.m. a lovely baby girl was safely delivered, and as Eve clamped and cut the umbilical cord Mrs Sayers kissed Melanie, laughing and crying at the same time. Outside in the corridor, Mr Sayers heard the piercing cry of the newborn child, and went into the waiting-room, where he sobbed his heart out, alone and unseen, for his daughter and granddaughter—and for his wife, whose life was going to be completely changed by this event.

Melanie did not need any stitches, and as soon as the placenta was expelled the baby was placed in her mother's arms by the new grandmother. In that moment, the plans for adoption were discarded.

Eve sighed, and momentarily closed her eyes. 'Right, Nancy, tea for everybody, please. We could all use a cuppa, I think.'

Annette reluctantly marvelled at the senior midwife's coolness and complete self-control. Her cap still sat straight and firm on her golden head, and her creamy complexion was only faintly flushed. The blue-black mascara was as immaculate as when she had come on duty.

As soon as she had swallowed half of the mug of freshly

brewed tea that Nancy poured out for her, Eve went into Stage One Room A to take Mrs Blair's pulse and blood-pressure and check that the epidural was working well. As she glanced at the foetal heart-rate recorded on the monitor she noted with concern that there were marked decelerations with each contraction. She picked up the oxygen mask attached to the fitted flow-meter, and, turning on the supply, she put the mask over Mrs Blair's nose and mouth, asking her to breathe the pure oxygen deeply.

'This is for your baby's benefit, my dear,' she said reassuringly as Mr Blair stared in dismay. Eve rang the call-bell, and Nancy came to answer it.

'Bleep Dr Roberts for me, will you?' said Eve in a low tone. 'Tell him we're getting type two dips here, though I think she's nearly ready to push.' Raising her voice, she told the couple, 'I'm just going to do a little internal examination to see where we're up to.'

Poor Mrs Blair, whose carefully written Birth Plan had included a request that there should be no foetal monitor-ing, no intravenous drip and no deliberate rupturing of her membranes, had by now completely entrusted herself and her baby to the care of the obstetric team—had done so when she had been forced to ask for an epidural anaesthetic, which automatically involved a precaution-ary drip and continuous foetal monitoring. She now willingly let Eve's fingers probe the rim of the cervix, and anxiously awaited the verdict.

'Almost there, my dear,' smiled Eve, withdrawing her hand, and suddenly there was a gush of thick dark green liquid in the bed. Eve's eyes turned to the monitor: the baby's heart-rate was dropping to below a hundred beats per minute—below ninety—down to eighty, and then slowly recovering to around a hundred between contractions.

Chris Roberts hurried in and gave a low whistle at the sight of the meconium-stained liquor, which, like the erratic heart-rate, indicated that the baby was in some distress.

'Get Dr Rowan, Chris,' muttered Eve, 'and alert Dr Grant and the paediatrician. We may need to go into theatre with Mrs Blair—no, no, don't worry, my dear, everything's all right, honestly—just be glad that you're here with us and all the facilities at hand to get you safely delivered as soon as possible.'

In less than two minutes Rowan appeared in the doorway, his white coat pulled over hastily donned trousers and shirt.

'Is she cross-matched?' he asked.

Chris nodded. 'Yes, there are two pints over in the blood bank.' He sighed with relief as he whispered to Eve, 'Call me superstitious, but I had a hunch that I ought to cross-match her when I saw that Birth Plan!'

Dr Grant, the anaesthetist, arrived, and after a brief consultation with Dr Rowan and the Blairs it was decided that he would top up the epidural anaesthetic, under which a Caesarean section would be performed. That meant that Mrs Blair would be conscious but pain-free throughout the operation, and her husband would be able to sit beside her, gowned and masked, in the theatre.

Chris got Mrs Blair to sign a 'Consent to Operation' form, which he witnessed, and Annette prepared her for Theatre, emptying her bladder with a plastic catheter, and dressing her in a theatre gown and cap. Her husband took charge of her rings and watch.

Meanwhile Eve and Rowan were scrubbing up in the theatre, and Nancy attired herself in the blue tunic and trousers of theatre 'runner'. Within fifteen minutes of discovering the warning signs of foetal anoxia, the operation was under way. Eve's composure never faltered as she handed the instruments to David Rowan across the table on which their patient lay, her baby's life in their hands. Eve's grey-green eyes watched in cool appraisal as Rowan extracted the baby from the mother's abdomen, unwinding the long cord which was tangled round its body, and holding it upside-down as Dr Laura Keene, the paediatrician, cleared its air passages with a mucus extractor. The cord was clamped and cut, and Dr Keene took the baby over to the resuscitation cot. A loud squeal went up from the newcomer, and everybody sighed with relief.

'Congratulations, Mr and Mrs Blair—you've got a fine son at twenty-five minutes past one,' said David, and the new father leaned over to kiss his wife in wordless, loving gratitude.

'Nice work, Dr Rowan,' observed Eve quietly as she prepared the thread for suturing the neat incision he had made in the abdomen and uterus, and which he now carefully proceeded to close, layer by layer.

'Bad quarter of an hour there, wasn't it?' he replied in an equally low voice. 'Did you see how the cord was wound tightly round the poor little chap's legs in a figure-of-eight? He must have been turning round like a whirling dervish in there. I could have got him out with a high forceps, I think, but on the whole I prefer Caesars—safer for the infant. Can somebody wipe my glasses? I'm all steamed up!'

Nancy deftly removed the horn-rimmed spectacles for about two seconds, wiped the inside with a piece of gauze and replaced them on his nose.

'Thanks. They're a nuisance in Theatre. Good job I

don't have to worry about my eye make-up, eh, Sister West? Yours must be very skilfully put on! All this heat and moisture, running around changing into theatre gear and back into uniform again, and never a lash out of place! They must call you No-Smudge West.'

The beautiful grey-green eyes met his in silent amusement above her sterile face-mask as she replied demurely, 'That's right, Dr Rowan. They do.'

With a healthily yelling baby in the cot, and an exhausted but overjoyed couple admiring their every move, the doctor and midwife felt able to relax a little and exchange some light-hearted banter. On completion of the operation, David Rowan pulled off his theatre gown, cap, mask and gloves, and stretched his broad shoulders.

'Thank you all very much indeed!' The words were uttered with genuine feeling. 'Quite frankly, I wasn't sure how I was going to make out in a completely strange set-up, but it went very smoothly, thanks to the excellent technique of—er—all the staff.'

'Oh, don't mention it, Dr Rowan!' simpered Nancy, with a wink in Eve's direction. 'It was nothing, really. Any time I can be of service to you——'

'That's enough nonsense from you, Nancy, my girl— go and put the kettle on!' ordered Eve, taking off her cap and running her hand over the smooth coil of her hair, from which a few stray tendrils were beginning to escape. Rowan stole a glance at her, and imagined unpinning that hair, watching the golden cascade fall over her shoulders. . .what's the matter with me? he thought.

As they sat over coffee in the office, writing up the details of the operation in the case-notes and register of births, he asked her if she lived in the adjoining nurses' home. She laughed.

'Good heavens, no! What do you take me for? I've got a rather nice flat out at Mill Green, about six miles out of Beltonshaw, over the Cheshire border.'

'I've rented a flat in Conway Road, not far from here,' he told her.

'Oh, yes? Is it nice?'

'It's convenient and will do as a bachelor pad for a couple of years. As you said earlier, Eve, I'll be either working here or studying for the fellowship, so I shan't need anything luxurious.'

He rose to his feet.

'I'd better get back and try to sleep for another hour or two. Thanks again, Eve—and thank you, Annette and Nancy. It's been great meeting you! Goodnight—er—good morning!'

'You know what? This could be the start of something big,' quipped Nancy as he lingered in the doorway. Nobody replied, and he hastily retreated down the corridor. Eve bent her head over the register, carefully filling in the columns so that a record of the Sayers and Blair births would be there for posterity.

In a few short hours, two total strangers had developed a close working relationship. And both of them were trying to tell themselves that it was all happening too quickly.

CHAPTER TWO

EVE'S tired brain was full of confused and contradictory thoughts as she drove out of Beltonshaw that Sunday morning, through the residential area and vast petrochemical complex that reared up like a science-fiction landscape in the cold grey light. Once on the main arterial road, she accelerated and sped between frosty fields and ragged hedges bordering farmland that had as yet escaped the creeping tentacles of Manchester overspill housing and industrial development. She usually felt a lightening of her spirits when she crossed the hump-back bridge that spanned a narrow waterway, for from there a vista of open countryside spread out before her; but this morning she hardly noticed the landmarks of the familiar journey. She was bothered by the memory of a pair of brooding dark eyes behind horn rims. . .and that intriguing accent, clipped but not a real South African twang—it was an accent that had travelled and picked up inflexions.

This was just too ridiculous, she told herself, making a conscious effort to dismiss the intrusive face and bring back to mind the image of the laughing fair-haired Philip Cranstone, whose blue eyes had turned towards her rather than to poor little Annette Gardner, who had so foolishly thrown herself at him when he had been the popular young houseman on the paediatric team. Philip was one of those happy characters whom everybody liked, who was always ready with a smile and a greeting, whether for his little patients on the children's ward and their parents, or the mothers on Post-Natal with their new babies. He was everybody's favourite doctor, and there was no denying that he was also rather a flirt: that was how he'd got entangled with Annette. Eve still felt uneasy when she remembered the hurt in the girl's eyes as the truth had dawned on her—that Philip did not after all return her adoration. Like many another man before him, he had been bewitched by Eve's sidelong glances, falling so quickly under her spell that he'd been called 'Eve's Golden Wonder-Boy' by some unkind observers. He'd wanted to get engaged before going on the course in paediatric cancers at Christie Hospital, but Eve had not wanted either of them to be committed until he had gained this valuable but very demanding experience, and was ready to apply for a registrar's post. At least, that was the explanation she had given him when she had refused to wear the diamond ring he had bought for her.

Annette Gardner would not have refused to wear it. Eve knew this, and the thought would not go away as she drove along the road beside the canal. Annette would have been proud to wear the ring and willing to wait for as long as fate decreed. . .because Annette had loved Philip, and loved him still.

These unwelcome reflections blended with the remembrance of David Rowan—damn the man, she'd only met him eleven hours ago! How thankful she was to reach Mill Green, a village still pleasantly rural in character, with its church, inn, post office and a few cottages nestling around the triangular green.

Set well back behind tall trees near the church was Jubilee House, once the home of a prosperous nine-teenth-century Lancashire cotton-mill-owner, and now converted into three flats whose tenants could enjoy the

spacious grounds. Garages had been built in place of the
old stables, and Eve drove the car into hers.

Her spirits lifted as they always did when she turned
the key of her door and entered the charming third-floor
flat. A substantial legacy from an aunt a few years
previously had enabled her to purchase this comfortable
home for herself and decorate it according to her own
taste. The furniture had come mainly from antique shops
and auction sales, and the pretty matching loose-covers,
curtains and cushions in a floral design gave the place a
cottage atmosphere, enhanced by the well-tended house-
plants in china and brass containers, standing on shelves
or suspended from wall-brackets. Through the half-
opened door of the pink and pale green bedroom a corner
of a rose-patterned duvet beckoned her with the promise
of peaceful sleep behind heavy velvet curtains that
excluded the daylight.

Eve kicked off her black duty shoes and looked round
with satisfaction at her sanctuary: it was the reason why
she stayed on at Beltonshaw General. Whatever gossip
might rage around her there, she could always return to
the seclusion of her lovely little home. And Eve West
knew about rumour and gossip—it had been a fact of her
life for a decade, ever since her parents had split up and
married new partners when she was an impressionable
sixteen-year-old, already the most attractive girl in the
school, and searching for security as well as love. Inevi-
tably she had been approached by boys and men, drawn
like moths to the flame of her blossoming beauty; how
easy it would have been for her to fall into the same
predicament as Melanie Sayers! That was why she always
felt so deeply for teenage mothers, though Eve had kept
her own emotions well under control, instinctively saving
herself for the man who could win her love. She had been

unable to resist a little playful teasing, leading men on as she discovered her growing sexual power—but there was an ice-maiden behind her smiling eyes, as more than one admirer had found out to his chagrin.

Then, at the age of twenty-two, Eve had fallen in love. As a newly qualified staff nurse, she had caught the eye of the consultant surgeon on whose male orthopaedic ward she had been given her first post. Mr Mason, in his mid-forties, had reached a static period in both his career and his marriage, and the beautiful girl with her long golden hair and demurely lowered grey-green eyes had fired his imagination. She for her part had gradually responded, and a tempestuous affair had resulted. Notes and phone calls had led to secret meetings, and Mason, though more than twenty years her senior and married with two teenage children, had become completely enchanted. He had sworn to her that he had never known a woman like her in his life, and that he could not live without her. Eve had clung to him: breathlessly she had listened, and all too willingly had she believed his promises when he had told her that his marriage was virtually over in all but legality. Trustingly she had given herself, and hospital gossip had been rife around them as she had waited for the news of his separation from his wife, and the commencement of divorce proceedings.

It had never come, thanks to some quick thinking and prompt action on the part of his wife, an underestimated lady who was prepared to fight to keep her husband and save their family life. Mr Mason had been forced to reconsider his position, and eventually he had sent Eve a letter, praising the happiness he had regained in marriage and fatherhood. He begged her to forget him and find a younger man who could offer the same security to her.

The effect upon Eve had been deeply damaging. Out

of her bitter disillusionment she had developed a compulsion to prove herself irresistible to every man who came her way, whether he was free to respond to her or not. Wielding her now almost legendary power to bewitch, she had acquired a reputation for being able to entangle any man she chose if she was sufficiently determined to do so. 'She can't live without a man': Sister Hicks's words had reflected the general consensus of opinion about Eve, but it was by no means accurate, the truth being that the ice-maiden had never again given herself to a lover. In her elegant prime at twenty-seven, with a good career that she enjoyed, Eve was a confident survivor, now as good as engaged to Philip Cranstone; she was looking forward to marriage and family life.

Or was she? Closing her eyes, she saw the face of the new obstetric registrar and heard again the words that had made her heart lurch: 'I do hope that we're going to have a good working relationship. . . I'd appreciate that.' Only a pleasant, friendly observation, nothing to get excited about, surely? And would he be deputising for Mr Andreasson again tonight?

I'm overtired, she told herself; my brain's feeling the strain of too many nights on duty at a stretch. I need a bath and a good sleep. Realising that she was also hungry, she went into the kitchen and plugged in the electric toaster.

The doorbell rang. It was Andrew Rayner from the flat below hers, overweight and over-friendly. A sales representative for a firm of baby foods and special diet preparations, he lived in hopes of getting to know his attractive neighbour better.

'Hi, Eve! Had a busy night?'

'Moderately.' He was obviously hoping to be asked in, but she was in no mood for listening to shop talk.

'Listen, you remember me telling you about that guy at Harrogate, the one who owns the chain of nursing homes? Guess what—I'm seeing him tomorrow, and it'll be a whopping commission if I pull off a deal. Wish me luck, Eve!'

She yawned. 'Yes, of course. Take him out to lunch and give him the full treatment on the expense account!'

'Are you off tonight?' he asked eagerly.

'No. One more to work, and then I'm off for three.'

'Great! How about a celebration dinner if I get the Harrogate contract—or even if I don't?'

'I'm sorry, Andrew, but I'm not sure what my plans are, so I can't commit myself,' she said evasively. 'Look, I'm feeling very tired right now——'

His face fell. 'Sorry. Well, wish me good luck in the customary way, then.'

And with annoying familiarity he leaned forward and planted a kiss on her cold cheek. She drew back.

'Goodbye, Andrew. Good luck!' And she closed the door firmly. Andrew Rayner was quite frankly a nuisance. He had moved into the flat below six months previously, and considered that their work gave them a common interest.

'What's a stunning girl like you doing as a *midwife*, for heaven's sake?' he'd asked incredulously when he'd found out her occupation. 'And tucked away on night duty, too! I thought you must be earning a fortune as a top model or something.'

'Why on earth does everybody think that all midwives are bossy middle-aged women as plain as pikestaffs?' she had answered crossly. 'I happen to enjoy my work immensely, thank you very much!'

As a too-close neighbour, he had constantly to be kept at bay, though on a couple of occasions she had accepted

an invitation to go out to dinner with him, allowing him
the privilege of escorting a woman who turned all heads
in their direction—but she seldom asked him into her
flat or entered his, in spite of his frequent attempts to
persuade her.

Sliding drowsily under the duvet after her bath, Eve
prepared to let the winter day pass in oblivion; but her
sleep was troubled by strange dreams and sudden awak-
enings, when she lay staring at the ceiling in unexplained
anxiety.

At six o'clock she got out of bed and put on the flowing
jellaba in which she always felt comfortable. In heavy
black cotton with a blaze of embroidery, it swirled
elegantly around her body as she went into the kitchen to
poach two eggs, preparing a tasty little meal on a tray.
Settling into an armchair, she turned on the television.

Just after seven the telephone rang. It was Philip
Cranstone.

'Are you all right, darling? I haven't got you out of
bed, have I?' he asked.

'No, of course not, Phil. I'm already up. How are
things with you these days?'

'Well, I'm finding it pretty heavy going, Eve. It's so
different from the paediatrics at Beltonshaw—there isn't
the same pace and tension, but the wear and tear on the
emotions is something else—oh, boy! I just can't begin
to describe it. You remember that little chap I told you
about, the one with the brain tumour? He had a second
operation yesterday, and I've been with him practically
non-stop, and so have his parents. It's too early yet to
know how successful it will be—or *not*—and somehow
or other I've got to help them to keep going without
raising their hopes too high. In any case, he'll need weeks

to learn to walk and talk again, even if the malignancy hasn't gone too far and doesn't recur. . .'

There was real distress in his voice as he continued to tell her about the boy, and Eve felt very uncomfortable as she listened. It was obvious that Philip was finding life very difficult at Christie's, and needed somebody to confide in, some close friend or counsellor to whom he could unburden the pain and the pity; he was genuinely fond of children, and they were drawn to his warm personality. What more natural than that he should turn to the woman he loved for comfort? And what had Eve to offer him?

'Oh, Phil, I'm terribly sorry not to be with you. I'd really like to hear all about your impressions—and feelings. Look, I'm on duty tonight, and then off Monday, Tuesday and Wednesday. Can we meet on one of those evenings?'

'Bless you, darling, I can hardly wait!' he replied fervently. 'Monday—that's tomorrow, a bit dodgy, but what about Tuesday? Shall I come over to your flat?'

'Er—yes, that would be fine, Phil. Let's make it Tuesday.'

'I honestly can't manage it tomorrow, worse luck.'

And I'll be tired out anyway, thought Eve, and not much use to him.

'Right, Phil,' she said, 'I'll have an early night tomorrow, and get a nice dinner ready for us on Tuesday. Come over to Mill Green as soon as you can get away, then.'

There was a long sigh at the other end of the telephone.

'The very thought of it will keep me going, my love.'

'Me too, Phil. Look, I must ring off now. I'm not even dressed for duty yet.'

'Sorry, Eve. It's such heaven just to hear your voice. Goodnight, darling. Goodnight, my beautiful——'

'Goodnight, Phil. Take care now, and I hope your little patient goes on well.'

And she hung up the telephone, unable to bear his need of her for another minute.

She put on her uniform and then sat down at the dressing-table for the fifteen-minute ritual of applying her make-up. She always found this soothing, almost therapeutic. However tired she felt, whatever headache or period discomfort she might experience, Eve West always paid scrupulous attention to her appearance. It was important to her that she should put a good face on the turmoil that might surge around her; she could hide her true feelings behind the lovely, composed mask that she showed to the world.

She smiled at her reflection when she had finished, and added a tiny dot of palest pink blusher, which she smoothed in with her fingers. But tonight she was unsatisfied with the face that smiled mechanically back at her. It had an anxious expression, with uncertainty in the eyes and a tension in the set of the mouth. What was the matter?

Philip Cranstone—'Eve's Golden Wonder-Boy'—*no*!

'Oh, my God,' she said aloud as the realisation came to her that she could not allow this pretence to go on any longer. She had acted wrongly and heartlessly in deliberately setting out to bewitch Philip; and she had worsened the situation by not refusing absolutely to become engaged. The ridiculous 'unofficial' understanding was a farce that meant so much more to him than to her.

'Poor Phil, I'm going to have to put a stop to this,' she said to herself wretchedly. She would have to tell him on Tuesday evening, face to face, that she could not marry him. She must not let him go on thinking that she returned his love.

Only now did she acknowledge in her heart that she was not in love with Philip Cranstone, and never had been. She had thought herself to be happy with the unofficial engagement, proud of her conquest and secure in the love of everybody's favourite doctor—until now. Until last night. It had taken a complete stranger to make her see that marriage to Philip would be a disastrous mistake. And she would have to tell him so, definitely and finally, on Tuesday evening, when he came to her for comfort and consolation. To use the old saying in sincerity and truth, she would have to be cruel to be kind.

Having made up her mind on this course of action, she was aware of a lightening of her heart and conscience, even though she dreaded the coming ordeal and the blow she would have to deal to Philip for the sake of his long-term happiness. And oh, how thankful she was that she had never yielded to his whispered entreaties when they had spent evenings together alone: something had always just held her back from complete surrender, and now she closed her eyes and sighed with relief for this at least.

Meanwhile tonight's work awaited her. . .and David Rowan.

CHAPTER THREE

'SURE, and it's a busy time ye've had while I've been away, Sister West,' said Miss Marie O'Casey, the night nursing officer for midwifery, back from attending a statutory refresher course. 'Ye seem to have coped very well, but I doubt ye're sorry that this is your last night on.'

'I've had good staff on with me,' replied Eve coolly. She had no intention of admitting to any difficulties, or even to feeling tired after a week of acting as nursing officer.

'Yes, little Staff Nurse Gardner's very good, and Sister Hicks is all right when she stops talkin',' observed Miss O'Casey, a short, prettily plump Irishwoman in her mid-forties who looked at least ten years younger. 'I see we've got a new student midwife on with us tonight, and a new medical student from the university. Let's hope there'll be deliveries for them both.'

'There could well be, seeing that there are two patients in labour already,' replied Eve, 'a primigravida of twenty-seven and a single girl of twenty, having her second. The first one's in care, and she also had an abortion when she was sixteen.'

'Oh, aye, I heard the report,' nodded Miss O'Casey. 'I'd like to take Student Nurse Kelsey for a delivery, just to see how she gets on, like, as I haven't come across her before. I'll send her to look after the primip in Stage One Room B, that's Mrs Cotterell. I believe ye went to school wid her, Sister.'

'Yes, she was in my year, and very arty,' said Eve, wondering how on earth the Irishwoman had known. When a midwife knew a patient personally she was not usually asked to take the delivery unless both she and the patient wished her to do so.

'You take that poor girl Tracy Datchett, who hasn't got anybody wid her except her sister, who's sittin' smokin' in the waitin'-room,' decided Miss O'Casey. 'The medical student can go in wid ye and get an idea o' your technique and general attitude, Sister.'

'Thank you,' said Eve briefly, realising that the bustling little Irishwoman was now back in charge, while she must be ready to take the orders. At the same time she mentally acknowledged the compliment implied in Miss O'Casey's last words.

'Grand! Let's go and introduce ourselves to the patients, and then we'll have a chat back here in the office wid the new girl and boy!' declared the nursing officer, tip-tapping briskly away down the corridor to the stage one rooms.

Eve hid her tiredness and slight headache behind a bright smile as she entered Stage One Room A. A thin-faced girl with smudged eye-liner and dyed, lifeless hair was sitting up in the bed, supported on a bank of pillows.

'Hello, Tracy! I'm Sister West, your midwife on duty tonight. I'll be here until eight o'clock in the morning, so I'm looking forward to delivering your baby some time during the night. How's it going? Are your pains getting stronger?'

'Yeah—but I'd be all right if I could have a cigarette,' muttered the girl. 'Any chance of getting out to the waiting-room for a quick smoke?'

'No, Tracy, I'm afraid not,' replied Eve sympathetically, noting the girl's nicotine-stained fingers. 'You'll be able to have one after you're delivered. Is your sister around?'

'Yeah, but she keeps going out for a smoke,' said Tracy gloomily.

Eve decided to have a word with Tracy's sister.

'I think I need the toilet,' said the girl, and Eve undid the abdominal straps which fastened the two monitoring sensors to Tracy, one recording the foetal heart and the other showing the strength and frequency of the contractions. Gently helping Tracy off the bed, she escorted her to the *en suite* toilet and waited for her; then, helping her back to bed, she reconnected the monitor. She then checked the patient's temperature, pulse and blood-pressure.

'I'll do an internal examination on you soon, Tracy, and then we'll have a chat about pain relief. By the way, would you mind if a medical student helped me to look after you in labour and during the birth of your baby?'

'Don't care who's around as long as I can get this lot over and have a smoke,' replied the girl ungraciously.

'Good! I'll be back soon, then,' said Eve, handing her a magazine which she knew contained a cigarette advertisement with the usual government health warning with reference to the effects on the unborn child. She sighed, unable to decide whom she pitied the most, the under-nourished girl or the soon-to-be-born baby. There were no anxious parents awaiting the arrival of a grandchild, no boyfriend at the bedside, only a bewildered sister of about seventeen, who obviously relied on Tracy to look after her. The sisters seemed to have nobody but each other to share their aimless, hand-to-mouth existence.

Back in the office, Miss O'Casey was talking to Annette, who was in charge of the ante-natal ward, and the student midwife, Nurse Pat Kelsey, a pleasant red-haired girl who was thrilled at the prospect of having her third normal delivery when Mrs Cotterell's baby arrived. A solemn young man with round spectacles nervously introduced himself as Selwyn Digweed, medical student. It was the practice of the University Hospital to 'farm out' its medical students to surrounding suburban hospitals in order to get at least ten normal deliveries each, plus experience of general obstetric practice at first hand—what was sometimes called 'hands on' midwifery, actual on-the-spot experience of mothers and babies in all their variety of social class, race, culture, physical type and intelligence.

'No two are ever alike, ye see,' Miss O'Casey explained to Pat and Selwyn. 'And let me tell you something, friendly in your ear, like—nobody can ever say for certain that a birth is goin' to be normal. Ye can only say that it *was* normal, when it's all over. Mother Nature is all very fine when she's in a good mood, and a normal delivery is what we all hope for—but the old lady isn't always kind, ye see, in fact she can suddenly turn into an old crow who won't co-operate wid your plans for the birth. Well, if that happens, ye don't run any risks wid your mother and baby. Ye need a doctor, and not just any doctor—ye need a qualified obstetrician and ye need him fast, right?'

'Well said! If they don't learn anything else tonight, your students have just had one important lesson!'

This comment was uttered in a deep voice with a clipped accent as the broad frame of Dr David Rowan filled the doorway. Eve felt her heart leap at the sight of the dark eyes which quickly met hers in a special smile of greeting.

'Hello again, Sister West. You'll have to introduce me to this wise Irish lady.'

Miss O'Casey looked up, an amused expression in her wide blue eyes. Eve coloured slightly as she smiled and briefly nodded from one to the other.

'Miss O'Casey, this is Dr Rowan, who is to be Mr Horsfield's registrar in place of Mr Andreasson. He has recently arrived from Johannesburg.'

The Irishwoman at once held out her hand, which was warmly grasped by the doctor towering above her.

'No need to say more, Eve,' he beamed. 'You must be the formidable Marie O'Casey! I'm very pleased to meet you. How was the refresher course?'

'Oh, the usual talkin' and layin' down the law from them wid all the fine theories about how we ought to do our work—and the usual dead silence from all the practical, down-to-earth midwives who actually deliver the babies,' she answered drily. 'It's always the same at these talkin'-shops. I can tell exactly who's just come from work in a busy maternity unit, and who's been writin' a lot of clever articles for the nursin' Press and women's magazines.'

'But surely you expressed *your* opinions, Miss O'Casey?' asked Rowan with a sideways look at Eve.

'Oh, ah, I said me piece, but I wasn't thanked for it, only a few "hear, hear"'s from the rank an' file sittin' in rows waitin' for the tea-break. But what about yeself, Dr Rowan? How does Beltonshaw General compare wid the fine big hospital ye've come from?'

His face looked suddenly grave as he picked up a mug of coffee from the tray.

'Difficult to say. I led two lives out there, Miss O'Casey.'

'Did ye now, Doctor? That must have been interestin' for ye!'

Although he was addressing the nursing officer, all the

staff listened with interest as he spoke of the life he had left behind.

'The modern maternity unit was everything you could wish for, and yes, maybe it had the edge on Beltonshaw,' he said. 'My professor of obs. and gynae. was terrific, and taught me most of what I know. But the African townships were another matter altogether. I started going out to bush clinics just for one day a week, but gradually that side of the work took over. If I'm going to compare this place with what those native women had by way of maternity services, well, this is a palace.'

His expression darkened, and Eve instinctively felt that he was not yet ready to say more about his past experiences.

'There are two patients in labour at present, Dr Rowan,' she said after a slight pause, and gave him brief details of Tracy Datchett, while Miss O'Casey asked Nurse Kelsey to report on the progress of Mrs Cotterell.

'She's relaxing quite well between her contractions, and is walking around with her husband, using the rocking-chair when she gets a pain,' said Pat. 'The cervix is about two centimetres dilated, and she thinks she'll want an epidural when the pains get really strong.'

He nodded. 'Good. Well, Selwyn, I leave you in capable hands, and it's up to you to learn all you can from the midwives. Have you had any deliveries yet?'

'Er—yes—er—no, I've witnessed a few,' stammered the young man awkwardly. 'I don't really feel quite ready yet to—er——'

'Don't ye be worryin', Mr Digweed, Sister West will look after ye when the poor Datchett girl delivers,' Miss O'Casey reassured him. 'Nurse Kelsey can deliver Mrs Cotterell if all goes well. If we get any more admissions in labour ye'll have to take it in turns.'

She turned her attention to Annette Gardner, who was making a list of her ante-natal patients on four-hourly blood-pressure and urine testing.

'I want a word wid ye, Staff Nurse, about Mrs Graham, the diabetic lady who's for a blood-sugar profile. Just fetch me her case-notes, will ye? Let me see, she's not due until April. . .'

As they studied Mrs Graham's history, Rowan turned to Eve, his dark eyes alive with interest and something more than just admiration of a beautiful woman.

'I've been thinking about your remarks last night about your flat, Eve,' he said, 'and I think I ought to do something about this flat I've rented in Conway Road. I'm going to spend a lot of time in it studying, and it might as well be made as pleasant as possible. Did you say you'd decorated your own place at Mill Green?'

Eve's eyes shone and her mouth curved in an understanding smile that caused Rowan to stare in renewed amazement. What a stunner this woman was! Had he come over from South Africa to meet his destiny? What madness had got hold of him?

'Yes, I've gradually gone through it, painting and papering in easy stages,' she replied, and he did not guess at the effort she was making to sound casual. 'I think it's most important to live in congenial surroundings, somewhere that reflects our own tastes in colour, design and so on. For my part, I find it absolutely essential to have a place of my own where I can relax and—well, just be myself.'

She looked at him, her grey-green eyes sparkling with gold glints. Miss O'Casey, in conversation with Annette and with her back to Eve and Rowan, was fully aware of their exchange.

'Look—er—I wonder if you would care to advise me

on the subject of decorating this flat of mine,' went on Rowan, his gaze fastened on those enchanting liquid depths. 'Perhaps at some time convenient to you, Eve, I could ask you to come round to Conway Road and take a look at the place. Your expert advice would be very much appreciated. . .'

'Have ye heard how Dr Cranstone's gettin' on at Christie's, Sister West?' came the clear tones of the Irishwoman, breaking in on their low voices.

'Yes, Miss O'Casey, he's been in touch with some of us here,' answered Eve promptly, turning away from Rowan and noticing how Annette Gardner had stiffened suddenly. 'I believe he's doing very well; he's always happy in the company of children, of course, though it's rather harrowing at times, I gather.'

She spoke in the tone of one who was a friend but not intimately close to the man they were discussing. Miss O'Casey gave her a sharp look.

'I don't doubt he finds it very hard, Sister,' she observed. 'Seein' as he is so fond o' children, it's goin' to be no easy matter for him to see little ones wid cancer, and some of them dyin'. A man like Dr Cranstone needs somebody to turn to, somebody who's ready to listen to him, comfort him, care about him, like. Don't you think so, Sister?'

Eve felt extremely uncomfortable as she murmured, 'Well, yes, of course,' and had to force herself to look straight at the nursing officer. But Miss O'Casey was directing her gaze towards Annette, who, with downcast eyes and painfully flushed cheeks, was apparently studying Mrs Graham's case-notes.

Rowan heard the exchange, and noted Annette's reaction. He also remembered Chris Roberts's remark the previous night, and how Eve had sharply replied that she

did not 'belong' to anybody. He therefore surmised that
this paediatrician must have been infatuated with Eve—
and what man would not be, for heaven's sake?—but
that she had found his attentions unwelcome; and it
looked as if little Staff Nurse Gardner would be more
than happy to fill the role that Miss O'Casey had just
been describing. He hoped that things would work out
for the staff midwife, who seemed a nice kid, but of
course Eve West outshone any other woman in her
company. And how!

He turned to resume his conversation with her, but
found that she had left the office to attend to Tracy
Datchett. Selwyn scuttled after her, anxious to get started
on his six weeks' practical obstetric experience and to
learn all he could from these cool, competent midwives
at Beltonshaw.

'Right, Miss O'Casey, I think I'll go over to the
residency now,' said Rowan. 'Everything seems to be
under control here. Give me a buzz, of course, if you run
into any——'

'Of course, Dr Rowan; goodnight,' she replied, and,
although her tone was perfectly polite, he had the feeling
that he was being dismissed. And he had not had the
chance to make a definite date with Eve to visit his flat.
Damn! With a final nod, he strode away.

Tracy made steady progress in labour, and at one-fifty
a.m. a flushed and perspiring Selwyn delivered her of a
baby girl weighing five and a half pounds, whose piercing
squeals drowned the quiet instructions that Eve whispered to him as she stood at his side.

'Well done! Good girl, Tracy! You've got a dear little
girl—that's right, Selwyn, cut the cord now—no, this
side of the clamp, that's the way—good! Now, young
lady,' she went on, addressing the baby, 'I've got a nice

warm towel here to wrap you in, and I'll hand you to your mummy for a cuddle—OK?'

'I don't think she'll need any stitches,' muttered Selwyn.

'No, the baby's small and came through easily,' Eve replied. 'Good work, Selwyn. We'll get the placenta out, and then it will be time for a cuppa all round—and mountains of paperwork for you and me!'

Meanwhile Mrs Cotterell had needed an epidural, and Miss O'Casey had recalled Dr Rowan because her contractions had become weak and infrequent. He had decided to rupture her membranes and add a uterine stimulant, syntocinon, to the intravenous drip that the anaesthetist had commenced when the epidural had been sited.

At half-past two David was more than ready to return to his bed in the residency, but, hoping for a word with Eve, he went into the office where she was showing Selwyn how to fill in the details of the delivery in Tracy's case-notes. The medical student's hand shook slightly with fatigue and excitement as he scribbled away at her dictation, unable to believe that he had delivered a baby at last. Eve leaned across his shoulder to point out one or two amendments to what he had written, and the polished pink nail of her forefinger underlined the printed boxes where the details of stages one, two and three had to be recorded.

'Put down that the placenta was small and infarcted, and weighed only four hundred and twenty grams,' she told him. 'Cord thin and stringy, membranes ragged but appeared to be complete.'

'Er—yes, Sister, thank you,' he mumbled, busily writing on the blue printed form under the heading 'Stage Three'.

'The fact that the baby is underweight at full term is a reflection of Tracy's poor diet and heavy smoking,' remarked Eve.

'It's terribly sad, isn't it?' he replied with a shake of his head.

David Rowan could sympathise with the serious-faced student as he regarded the soft roundness of Eve's arms and the pink-tipped fingers holding the pen. My God, if the sight of this woman's hand and arm has this effect on me, what chance would I have against the full battalions? he thought, then immediately composed his face as she looked up at him, the corners of her mouth curving in a questioning smile, her unpainted lips inviting. . .it was now or never, he decided.

'Oh, by the way, Eve, I see from your duty roster that you're off tonight. Have you got any plans for this evening?'

'Not that I can think of,' she answered coolly, lowering her lashes and adding a written comment to the case-notes.

'In that case, I wonder if you'd care to take a look at the flat, as we were saying earlier. I'm free tonight, too, and, if you've got nothing better to do than drop in on a bachelor's pad and maybe suggest a few improvements, maybe we could have dinner——'

He hesitated, wondering if the medical student was listening. There was a slight pause before Eve replied lightly, without looking up, 'Let's make it about eight, shall we, Dr Rowan?'

'That'd be fine. Shall I come over to Mill Green and collect you?' he asked with a slight breathlessness.

'No, it'll be so dark, and you don't know the way. I'll drive over and meet you here at the front car park,' she told him.

'Great. All right, then, Sister West, it's time I tried to get some beauty sleep. I think Mrs Cotterell will go ahead and deliver normally. Call me if she doesn't,' he added with sudden briskness, aware that Miss O'Casey's neat, uniformed figure had appeared at the office door. 'Goodnight, then, ladies—or, rather, good morning!'

'Good mornin' to ye, Doctor,' replied the Irishwoman, who had heard every word.

CHAPTER FOUR

AFTER Mr Horsfield's round of his maternity patients on Monday morning he complimented Dr Rowan on the way he had coped with the obstetric emergencies of the weekend. The new registrar had performed the Caesarean section on Mrs Blair, and had also carried out a forceps delivery and a Vantouse vacuum extraction. Three other patients that he had been called to see had responded well to the treatment he had ordered for them, and had progressed to normal births conducted by midwives. One of these had been Mrs Cotterell, delighted with the fine big baby girl that Nurse Kelsey had delivered under Miss O'Casey's supervision. The weekend had been quiet on the gynaecological ward, where there had been no operations and only one emergency admission, a threatened miscarriage.

'I think we shall work together well, Rowan,' remarked the consultant. 'We seem to be on the same wavelength in our approach to obstetrics. Safety first, eh?'

'Thank you, sir. I've certainly enjoyed the weekend,' smiled the registrar, looking down respectfully at the slightly stooping shoulders of the older man, who wore an impeccably tailored suit and peered shrewdly over the top of gold-rimmed half-moon spectacles.

'Watch your attitude with the midwives, though,' cautioned Mr Horsfield. 'Smooth and friendly team-work is absolutely essential at all times, and never forget that they deliver at least three-quarters of our patients—so they can be said to run the service.'

David Rowan nodded.

'You get to know the ones you can safely leave in charge, Rowan, the ones who'll call you for a good reason—and always go to the department *at once* when you're called.'

'Well, naturally, sir. Any of us would, surely!' protested David in some surprise.

'Not always,' came the gruff reply. 'I nearly lost a baby once because a registrar tried to conduct the delivery by remote control, from his room. He was summoned twice by Miss O'Casey, and gave her instructions over the phone, if you please. She then telephoned me at my home, thank heaven.'

David shuddered inwardly at the thought of that registrar's disgrace. The consultant suddenly looked up at him, adjusting the half-moons on his nose.

'By the way, Rowan, I wonder if I could ask you to stay on call for one more night? Your opposite number is going to represent me at a college conference in London tomorrow, so he could do with a good night's sleep beforehand. I don't want to leave Beltonshaw just now; my wife's getting over an operation. Do you mind? I trust you haven't made any arrangements for tonight?'

'No, of course I'll stay on call, sir,' said Rowan promptly, while inwardly he cursed his luck. Damnation! He would have to cancel his date with Eve West. However, he hid his feelings, knowing that this request at such short notice was a test of his suitability for Mr Horsfield's team. It was well known that the consultant was hoping to cut down on his work at Beltonshaw General as he neared retirement, and to concentrate on his work as a lecturer and examiner for the Royal College and also for the midwives' central council; and it was understood that he was looking out for a worthy junior consultant. Once David Rowan had passed his fellowship examinations he knew that he would be very interested in being considered for this appointment. He had already decided that he liked Beltonshaw General, and one beautiful midwife in particular. . .

'Good, that's settled, then. Thanks.' Mr Horsfield picked up his briefcase and took out his car keys. 'I'll see you in the ante-natal clinic at two, Rowan.'

David Rowan smiled in agreement, concealing his irritation, and wondering when best to telephone Eve with the disappointing news that her visit to Conway Road would have to be postponed.

The busy clinic dragged on for nearly three hours; when it ended, David Rowan spent some time dictating letters to Mr Horsfield's secretary, and was then called to CDU to see a young woman who had been admitted because she thought her waters had broken two months before her first baby was due.

'I just felt this gush of water leaking out of me while I was going round the supermarket, Doctor!' she told him as he carefully questioned her in the admission room.

'The nitrazine test on this lady is negative, Dr Rowan,' said Sister Pardoe, the midwife on duty. This indicated that the membranes had not ruptured.

After a gentle speculum examination, Rowan told the girl, Wendy Clark, that he thought her waters were intact, but that he would like her to stay in overnight for rest and observation.

'You may have a touch of infection in your waterworks, Wendy. I'll ask Sister to send a specimen of your water and a vaginal swab to the laboratory, and we'll book you for an ultrasonic scan tomorrow. You haven't any pains, your baby's heartbeat is fine, and I don't think there's anything to worry about. However, we'll see how you are in the morning, and take it from there.'

'Well, thank you, Doctor, but I was *sure* that I was starting in labour!' said Wendy doubtfully, feeling that she had better not argue with the big, deep-voiced, rather stern-looking obstetrician. He wrote a few comments in her case-notes. Wendy Clark: later he would have cause to remember her name. . .

It was half-past six when he picked up the telephone in the residency and dialled Eve's number. He got an engaged signal, and continued to hear the irritating peep-peep-peep every time he dialled. Surely Eve could not be talking for over an hour! In actual fact, there was a fault on the Mill Green line, cutting off all incoming calls until engineers were sent out to repair it.

Exasperated after his latest attempt to get through, at seven-fifteen David showered and changed, ready to meet Eve at eight as planned. They would not be able to go to his flat while he was on call, but he decided to take her to the Irving Arms, a large and attractive pub opposite the front entrance and well frequented by hospital staff. With his bleep in his pocket, he thought he would be near enough to dash across the road and pick up the telephone at the porter's information desk if he was summoned.

As ill-luck would have it, the dark February sky erupted in a sudden downpour of rain as he saw Eve's small red saloon drive into the front car park. He ran to meet her as she emerged from it, and, taking her arm, he propelled her through the bucketing rain to the nearest entrance, Accident and Emergency.

'My dear Eve, I'm terribly sorry, but the great man has asked me to stay on call tonight,' he apologised. 'I tried to ring you several times, but——'

He stopped in mid-sentence as she smiled up at him, a radiant vision in a pale grey trench coat, her flawless complexion glistening with raindrops, her eyes sparkling and her blue-black lashes immaculate as always.

'Don't worry,' she reassured him, inwardly thankful that he had not been able to contact her. Just to be with him was everything.

'I—I thought we could go to the Irving, but it's raining cats and dogs,' he said with a grimace as they skirted the A and E reception and made for the main hospital corridor.

'You shouldn't leave the hospital, David. The residency has got a canteen with a bar,' she pointed out in a deliciously teasing tone.

'Yes, but that's no place to take a girl to dinner!' he protested, laughing in spite of his annoyance. 'Look, I could ask for some sandwiches and a drink to take to my room——'

'Why not ring for a Chinese? There's a very good one in Beltonshaw that will deliver to the residency,' she suggested. Eve knew that she was looking at her best after a good sleep during the hours of daylight, and her heart fluttered at the thought of a tête-à-tête meal in David's room. She was experiencing a truly new sensation tonight, and there were rainbows round her golden head. She was in love, and she knew it.

'What a splendid idea! Eve, you're a marvel! Come on, let's go through to the back exit and make a dash for it,' he grinned, responding to her light-hearted mood as they linked arms.

From the back of the hospital a laughing couple could be seen running from the covered passageway through the deluge towards the ground-floor entrance to the doctors' on-call quarters. He opened the door, and, as she preceded him into the light, their faces could be clearly seen for a moment, and the sound of their laughter echoed across the driveway at the back of the main hospital building.

A short, bouncy figure was hurrying out of the rear car park, an umbrella held aloft. She stopped for a moment to observe their faces before the door shut and hid them from her eyes and ears.

'Jesus, Mary and holy St Joseph! She hasn't wasted any time bewitchin' this one!' she said to herself, shaking her head as she continued on her way towards the covered passageway leading to the maternity department entrance. The night nursing officer was always early reporting for duty.

Rowan's room in the residency was very plainly furnished, with a single divan bed, two chairs and a small table upon which an Angle-poise lamp provided a subdued light. He had switched off the overhead light, and they now sat together on the tartan blanket which covered the bed and turned it into a divan settee. The discarded plastic plates and glasses from their Chinese meal were pushed aside on the table.

Call it love at first sight, fate or destiny, Eve thought in amazement, she only knew that she was drawn towards this man in a way that was completely new to her. This was no mere desire to bewitch; this was not just another name to add to her string of conquests: this was something totally different. She wanted to spend her life with this man, to share every part of his own life, to support him in his career, to create a home that they could share—quite simply, she wanted to become his wife and bear his children.

Joy and hope and love and fear—she felt them all as his

dark eyes fastened upon her, and her heart pounded when she saw the desire in their depths. They were both swept up and borne along on the tide of their mutual longing, and neither of them quite knew how to cope with it.

Rowan continued to gaze at his visitor, now curled up with her feet tucked under her lithe body, her back against the plain white wall. She wore a soft wool jersey dress in lavender-blue, and her hair was loosely caught with a comb at the back of her head. David wanted to release it and let it cascade over her shoulders, but he hardly dared move. Outside the rain continued to fall relentlessly, and suddenly there was a flicker of light at the window, followed by a distant growl of thunder. Eve shivered.

'Don't say you're afraid of thunder, my dear,' he whispered, putting a hand lightly on her shoulder.

'Of course not. I've always enjoyed a storm,' she answered, and he caught his breath at the golden glints in the grey-green eyes turned upon him. How could he resist her?

'Eve—it's nearly midnight. You really ought not to be here now,' he muttered in a voice that did not seem to belong to him. 'I mean, you know that I couldn't—oh, Eve, you beautiful woman. . .'

She nestled against his shoulder. Her mouth invited his kiss, her moist pink lips parted softly for him. How could he not touch her? How in God's name could he——? His thoughts were lost in the long, deep, all-absorbing kiss, which took away all caution. There was no past and no future, only the incredible present moment.

'Eve. . .lovely, lovely Eve. . .'

He gently withdrew himself from her softly clinging arms, and got up to turn the key in the lock. Settling back again on the divan, they heard another clap of thunder above the roaring torrent of rain. A distant window rattled, and there was a crash outside in the corridor.

'Hell, Eve, that will be the window that doesn't shut properly. I'm sorry, but I'd better go and close it,' he apologised.

Out in the corridor, he found the window open, curtains waving wildly, and rain driving in. A small table with a potted plant had been knocked over, and Rowan stood it upright again. He climbed up on to it and closed the window, clicking the catch firmly into place. Shaking the raindrops from his hair, he returned to his room. Opening the door, he stopped and stared in fresh incredulity at the woman on his bed. Her golden hair was loose on her gleaming shoulders: she had unbuttoned the front of her dress, and her arms were outstretched towards him.

This had to be a dream. He closed the door behind him, and went to her, burying his face in the warm sweetness of her throat and neck, sinking, drowning. Eve gave a long, shivering sigh.

Staff Nurse Gardner was collecting cups from her patients in the ante-natal ward at nearly midnight. This was because Miss O'Casey had asked Nancy to make tea for all the patients who had been awakened by the thunder. The storm had now passed over, but the rain continued to fall steadily. Balancing the tray on one arm, Annette softly closed the ward door and made her way to the kitchen. There she jumped violently at the sight of the dark, drenched figure before her, nearly dropping the tray on the floor.

'Steady, Annette! It's only me! I thought I'd pop in and beg for a hot drink. What a night!'

'Philip! Oh, Philip, how are you?' she cried in delight.

'So-so. It's good to see you again, Annette love. Look, I've been over to Mill Green and Eve's not at home. She wasn't expecting me tonight, but I managed to get away, and I—oh, Annette, what you women do to us poor fellows!' he sighed.

'Sister West isn't on duty tonight, and I don't know if she had any plans to——' Annette said coldly, then stopped, remembering the talk in the office the previous night. But Dr Rowan was on call, so Eve couldn't have gone to his flat in Conway Road. The girl shrugged, and then smiled brightly at the man she loved.

'Let me make you a drink and a sandwich, Philip, and dry those wet clothes!' she begged.

'Merciful heaven!' exclaimed Miss O'Casey, arriving at the door of the kitchen. 'Whatever brings ye here on such a dark and stormy night, Dr Cranstone? Sister West isn't on duty,' she added slyly.

'I know. Sorry, Miss O'Casey. I've just looked in to see you all, and——'

'Ah, I see that Staff Nurse is makin' ye a drink. That's good,' nodded the Irishwoman approvingly. 'Now, we all want to hear about Christie Hospital and how ye're gettin' on there!'

At that moment a call-bell rang in the ante-natal ward.

'All right, Staff Nurse, you carry on seein' to poor Dr Cranstone, and I'll answer the bell,' said Miss O'Casey quickly.

Annette poured out a cup of hot chocolate and buttered two slices of bread, adding cheese and tomato from the refrigerator. Her pale cheeks glowed with pleasure at

Philip's gratitude. As he began to tell her about his new job Miss O'Casey returned, frowning slightly.

'It's this girl Wendy Clark, Staff Nurse,' she said. 'It seems she was scared out o' her wits by the two claps o' thunder, and now she says she's gettin' pains. That girl's determined to go into premature labour! I don't think she's really contractin', but I'll fetched her out into Stage One Room B and put the monitor on her for a bit. No, no, *I'll* do it, you stay and talk to poor Dr Cranstone!'

Philip and Annette smiled shyly at each other as she bustled away. Presently she returned to the kitchen with a very thoughtful expression, and spoke to Annette in a low tone.

'Sure and I'm wonderin' if I should call up Dr Rowan to see her, Staff Nurse. It was himself who examined her when she came in, thinkin' her waters had gone.'

Annette was surprised.

'Won't you wait and see what the monitor picks up, Miss O'Casey? It doesn't really seem necessary to call out a registrar if we're not sure whether she's even contracting or not.'

'Well, now, ye could be right, Staff Nurse, but I'm thinkin' maybe he should see her sooner than later,' replied Miss O'Casey cryptically. 'After all, he gets paid good money to be on call, and we can't be takin' risks wid a thirty-two-weeker.' She paused and put her head on one side, her bright eyes narrowing with the effort of making a decision.

'Staff Nurse, I'm goin' to call him,' she said at last with resolution in her voice. Going into the office, she picked up the telephone and dialled three digits.

'Hello—will ye bleep me Dr Rowan for CDU?' they heard her say. She replaced the receiver and waited for a minute, then lifted it again.

'Hello. Dr Rowan hasn't answered his bleep. Will ye call him again, please?'

Another minute passed, and the phone did not ring. Miss O'Casey came out of the office, looking strangely flushed and perturbed. Her usually confident tones sounded a little strained as she turned to Philip.

'Dr Cranstone, seein' that ye're here, could I ask a favour of ye? Seemingly Dr Rowan's bleep isn't workin', and I wonder—could I possibly ask ye to go over to the doctors' on-call quarters in the residency, and tell him we want him here on CDU?'

'Why, of course, Miss O'Casey, no problem,' answered Philip in his friendly way. 'Do you know his room number? It'll be on the board over there, anyway. I'll go straight away!'

'It'll be Mr Andreasson's old room,' said Annette, still wondering why Miss O'Casey thought it necessary to disturb the registrar at this hour over a matter which could hardly be called an emergency. She was behaving very oddly tonight, thought Annette as the nursing officer snapped her fingers nervously as she tip-tapped to the stage one room and back again to the office.

'Is anything the matter, Miss O'Casey?' Annette timidly enquired. 'Do you want me to do anything for you?'

'Yes, yes, Staff Nurse, away wid ye and do a round of your patients!' the Irishwoman replied sharply.

Annette did as she was told, even though she had not long left her ward full of sleeping patients. When she had ascertained that they were all settled she returned to the kitchen, where Philip's drink and half-eaten sandwich remained on the work surface. Nancy came in with a couple more empty cups.

'What's up with the boss tonight?' she whispered to Annette. 'Don't tell me *she* was scared of the thunder!'

'Oh, Nancy, guess who's come to see us!' cried Annette, unable to hide her pleasure. 'Philip Cranstone!'

'Has he? Oh, great! Where is he?' asked Nancy eagerly.

'Miss O'Casey's just sent him over to the residency to call Dr Rowan to see Wendy Clark. His bleep's not working,' replied the innocent Annette.

Nancy stared. 'Oh, no,' she breathed.

'Why, what's the matter, Nancy?'

'Oh, no. Let me be wrong,' muttered the auxiliary, who had seen Eve's red saloon in the front car park.

Philip dashed along the first-floor corridor of the residency.

'Number twenty-one—twenty-two—twenty-three— ah, here it is,' he murmured, stopping at Number twenty-four. He rapped on the door.

'Dr Rowan! Dr Rowan, are you there?'

There was no reply, though Philip thought he might have heard a muffled exclamation.

'Rowan! You're wanted on CDU!' he called out more loudly. He tried the door: it opened, and he stepped into the room. The Angle-poise lamp was still on, and by its light he saw them.

'Rowan. . .! Oh.'

The words froze on Philip's lips as he stood and stared at the two figures on the divan. They were motionless, as if carved in stone. Eve was in her underslip, one lacy white strap pulled over her shoulder. David had discarded his shoes, spectacles and tie, and his shirt was unbuttoned. They both stared back at Philip, whose face had gone as white as the wall.

David Rowan recollected himself, and rose quickly from the divan.

'Er—hello. Did you say I was wanted on CDU? Why couldn't they bleep me? Right, I'll be over in two minutes, OK?' he said briskly and dismissively, expecting that the stranger would leave at once.

But Philip Cranstone turned a stricken gaze on Eve. 'You—you, Eve——' The sound was incoherent, an unbelieving groan. 'You and I—we're getting married, Eve—married!'

Rowan looked from one to the other. Eve was pulling on her dress as rapidly as she could, and making an effort to keep calm. Philip looked like a man who had just been stabbed. He swayed slightly, and put a hand on the doorframe as he continued to stare at her.

'No, Philip, we were never engaged,' said Eve in a low, breathless tone. 'I never wore your ring. Look, Philip, I'm terribly sorry, but you——'

'We were engaged as far as I was concerned!' Philip's colour began to return as he accused her.

'Good God, you must be Cranstone, the paediatrician!' exclaimed David, hastily putting on his shoes and fastening his shirt. 'Look, my dear chap, I can't tell you how sorry I am about this. I didn't realise that you were actually engaged to her, honestly I didn't. I'm sorry,' he repeated.

'Don't bother, Rowan,' replied Philip with a mirthless laugh. 'You're the one I'm sorry for. She didn't take long with you, did she? You're not the first, and you won't be the last. She's a——'

'*No*, Philip, it's not like that!' cried Eve as tears of shock and shame began to spill down her white face.

'Oh, careful, you'll spoil your make-up, darling,'

mocked Philip with terrible sarcasm. 'I suppose I should be thanking my lucky stars for finding out in time.'

'*No*! I was going to tell you tomorrow night!' pleaded Eve, now shaking in every nerve as the full implications of this hateful scene began to dawn on her.

'Oh, save your breath, Eve. I'll tell Miss O'Casey you're on your way, Rowan. Goodnight!'

And Philip was gone, leaving devastation behind him.

'David, you must believe me. I *was* going to tell him tomorrow night. I'm not in love with him. I never was.'

Rowan turned on her with a look of such blazing fury that she shrank back against the wall.

'Spare me the explanations. I had been told about you, Sister West, but I didn't believe it. You're quite a name to conjure with in the doctors' mess! I heard about the consultant surgeon whose marriage you tried to break up. I heard about Eve West's "Golden Wonder-Boy", but I was fool enough to think that poor Cranstone had just been infatuated with you, and that you'd turned him down. Oh, I didn't believe any of it, and now it seems that I'm the latest fly to be caught in your web!'

'David, please give me a chance to explain——'

'Look, I've got to see this patient. You are to get yourself dressed and out of this room before I return. This will be all over the hospital tomorrow, and Mr Horsfield is going to be vastly impressed, I'm sure. I intend to face this out, and have no more social contact with you whatsoever. So long, Sister West!'

'*David*! Please——'

But he was gone, leaving Eve feeling more wretched and ashamed than she had ever felt in her life before. Hauling on the trench coat and picking up her bag, she left the room and crept quietly out of the residency. The rain was abating as she walked round the hospital to the front car park and got into her little saloon. All she longed for now was the privacy of her flat in Jubilee House, her home and place of refuge. There she could weep and nurse her wounds like an injured animal, alone.

Dr Rowan examined Wendy Clark and soon decided that she was not in premature labour. He suspected that hers was a case of wishful thinking, that she simply wanted to have the baby and so bring her pregnancy to an early end. He spoke firmly to her, pointing out the risks to the child being born prematurely, and advising her to think positively, accepting the fact that she had another two months to nourish her baby and allow it to reach normal size and development.

After talking to Wendy Clark, Dr Rowan rang the bleep service of the hospital switchboard, and asked a question. It was answered.

'I'd like a word with you in the office, please, Miss O'Casey,' he demanded when he had replaced the receiver.

'Why, of course, Doctor. What can I do for ye?' Her wide blue eyes looked up innocently for a moment, but when she saw his grim expression she dropped her gaze and stared hard at Wendy's case-notes.

'Did you really try to bleep me twenty minutes ago?' he asked.

She was silent.

'I said, did you really try to bleep me, Miss O'Casey?'

The little Irishwoman looked up at him with regret in her eyes, though she spoke calmly and quietly.

'I'll have to go to Confession over this, Doctor, so I mustn't make it worse by tellin' a lie.'

He gave her a long look, and his expression relaxed. He looked utterly exhausted.

'Thank you, Marie. I suppose I ought to feel grateful

to you, but right now I'm afraid I don't. I just feel like one hell of a fool.'

She saw pain as well as anger in his pale face.

'I doubt ye feel as badly as the other two, Doctor— and remember that a nine days' wonder only lasts nine days. It gave me no pleasure to hurt me best midwife on night duty. No pleasure at all.'

And the little Irishwoman tip-tapped out of the office. Nancy, listening outside the door, had to move smartly to avoid a collision.

CHAPTER FIVE

EVE scarcely stirred from her flat during the rest of her three nights off duty, and the two long winter days between them. She felt that she had been utterly crushed under the weight of her humiliation, and the anger and contempt in Rowan's eyes. She knew that hospital gossip would be raging round her once again, and that Dr Rowan might well be reprimanded by Mr Horsfield over such an embarrassing incident so early in his registrarship on the consultant's team. It could jeopardise his future prospects, and it was all her fault. She wanted to curl up under her rose-patterned duvet and never emerge again. . .

'Eve West can't live without a man. . .'

She remembered Sister Hicks's words that she had overheard. Even her nursing colleagues thought she was a—the word that Philip Cranstone had nearly said during that shameful scene. How could she ever return to duty and face them all again? Miss O'Casey, Annette, Doris Hicks, the student midwives who would giggle behind her back—and David Rowan. How thoroughly demeaning her behaviour must appear to them all! No, she could not go back again after this. She would have to leave Beltonshaw and get a midwifery post in another part of the country. Or maybe she would go abroad—perhaps join one of the armed services in a nursing capacity. It would mean selling up and leaving this dear little flat, her refuge and hideaway. And she had only herself to blame!

Eve buried her face in her pillow and wept bitterly before falling into a merciful sleep of utter exhaustion.

On the Wednesday morning the telephone rang soon after nine. Eve picked up the receiver with a sense of foreboding.

'Hello.'

'Good mornin' to ye, Sister West. I'm just ringin' to ask if ye're feelin' better now, that's all.'

'Miss O'Casey—er—yes.' Eve hesitated at first, then found her voice. 'Thank you, I'm fine,' she lied.

'Good. I thought ye looked very tired when ye went off duty last. Have ye had a good rest, Sister?'

'Yes, I'm—I'm fine,' repeated Eve, as with a sinking heart she realised that the nursing officer must have heard all. Then a suspicion which had been forming at the back of her mind now leapt to the foreground at a single stroke.

Miss O'Casey had sent Philip Cranstone to Rowan's room *deliberately*, knowing what he would probably find.

'I'm very glad to hear that ye're all right, Sister. Now, will ye be able to report for duty again tomorrow night, or would ye like to take the rest of the week off? I'd be happy to work through to the end of this week if ye need a little more rest, like.'

It was decision time. Eve heard herself saying, 'Thank you, but I shall return to my work tomorrow, as shown on the duty roster.' Her voice was firm, clear and cold.

'Well done!' The nursing officer's voice was warm and friendly by contrast. 'Ye're me best midwife, Eve, and I'd be sorry to lose ye.'

Miss O'Casey seldom used Christian names when talking to her staff; her meaning was unmistakable, but Eve could not respond with the same degree of familiarity.

'Thank you for ringing, and I shall be on duty tomorrow at eight-thirty p.m.,' she said, hanging up. She had committed herself, and did not know whether she had made the right decision or not.

When she awoke on the Thursday morning, and drew back the velvet curtains, the sky was clear and the world looked newly washed after the rain. Below her window she could see the snowdrops which had pushed their fragile white heads up through the frosty earth. There was one golden crocus in bloom: soon there would be a carpet of them, in gold and white and mauve around Jubilee Hall. The earth was stirring, and getting ready for another spring.

Eve opened the window fully, and took a long, deep breath. She thought of the mothers who would be waiting for her skill and experience: the happy couples like the Blairs and Cotterells, the sad girls like Melanie Sayers and Tracy Datchett. She thought of all the babies she had brought into the world, and the gratitude she had received from patients and their relatives. She seemed to hear them calling out to her.

'Sister! Can you come at once, please!'. . . 'Oh, help me, Sister!'. . . 'It's a boy, Sister!'. . . 'Is my little girl all right, Sister?'. . . 'Thank you, Sister, oh, thank you!'

Tears began to roll down Eve's cheeks again, but these were different from the shameful floods of the last two days. She looked up at the bright blue sky and made a promise.

I'll go back to my work, and I'll stay on in my job, she resolved. If nobody else thinks I'm any good, my patients do. I've lost the only man I thought I could really love, and he thinks I'm the dregs—but I'm still a midwife, and a good one!

With this decision made, she braced herself and called

on all her reserves of courage. David had said that he intended to face this out, and so would she.

Whatever misfortune might befall her, Sister Eve West was a survivor.

That memorable February eventually came to an end, with a noticeable lengthening of the days; March came in with soft breezes and a few early daffodils in the grounds of Beltonshaw General Hospital.

Eve discovered that life went on, and that babies continued to be born, regardless of events in the lives of the staff; most of her colleagues behaved as if nothing had happened, and she was warmed by their friendliness. Only David Rowan was cold and distant.

At half-past seven one morning early in March, Eve dashed into the office to tackle the paperwork following a very busy night; there were dark shadows under her eyes, and her mouth tightened slightly at the recollection of Dr Rowan's silence as he had performed an emergency Caesarean section, accepting the instruments from her gloved hands without so much as a glance of acknowledgement. She turned to Nurse Kelsey, who was seated at the desk, writing up the case-notes of the mother she had delivered under Eve's supervision.

'You'd better transfer your patient and her baby to Post-Natal,' said Eve. 'We need the delivery room clear for the day staff to use.'

'Do you want me to take her down *now*?' asked the student midwife rather reluctantly, looking down at the pile of paperwork.

'Yes, right away,' answered Eve firmly. 'Patients first, paperwork second. The nursing auxiliaries are busy with the breakfasts. Let me know when you need a hand with the stretcher trolley.'

Pat Kelsey left the office, and Eve sat down in the vacated chair, taking her red and black Biro pens out of the top pocket of her dress.

A shadow loomed at the office door, and she looked up quickly, her fingers tensing on the pen she held. The familiar tall, broad figure of David Rowan stood in the doorway, and she was conscious of his impersonal, unsmiling glance behind the heavy horn-rims. His face, like hers, was pale with fatigue. Eve did not greet him, but waited for him to speak first.

'Good morning again. I thought the day staff would be here by now,' he observed in his clipped accent.

'Sister Pardoe should be here any minute now,' replied Eve coldly, bending her fair head over her paperwork and wondering what could have brought him back to the delivery unit: she had not sent for him. She continued to write in silence, thankful that he was unaware of the disturbing effect he had on her concentration and pulse-rate.

Nancy put her head round the door.

'Cup of tea, Sister West?' she offered as she wheeled the drinks trolley along the corridor.

'No, thank you, not just now,' answered Eve without looking up.

'What about you, Dr Rowan?' asked Nancy.

'Not for me,' he replied quickly, though he would have accepted one if Eve had done so. The little clatter of cups would have relieved the silent tension between them.

Instead they had to wait for the arrival of Sister Pardoe, a pleasant-faced Scotswoman in her forties.

'Good morning! Busy night?' she asked as she adjusted her white cap on her neat greying head.

'Morning, Sister Pardoe,' said Eve. 'I believe Dr Rowan wants to speak to you.'

'Trouble on Gynaecology, I'm afraid, Sister,' he said in answer to the older woman's questioning look. 'A patient has developed a post-op thrombosis, and she'll need to go on continuous heparin for a while. Could they borrow your Handley pump until they can get one from the stores?'

'Of course,' replied Sister Pardoe, adding with a smile, 'Have you got a new job as a porter, Dr Rowan? Couldn't they have sent an auxiliary over for it?'

'Well, I've got to kick around until the lab. technician phones back with the report on her blood samples before we can start pushing in the heparin,' he explained, his sombre features softening as he spoke to Sister Pardoe. 'And all the gynae. staff are busy preparing the theatre cases for today. Mr Horsfield's got a long list.'

He turned to find Eve at his elbow, holding the handbag-sized plastic box which contained the apparatus he required.

'There's an extension cannula in there, and a sixty-millilitre syringe,' she said crisply.

'Thank you—er—Sister West,' he replied with a nod, taking the box from her. As he went to the door he nearly collided with Sister Fay Mitchell coming on duty. She was a lively, petite girl of twenty-five, in charge of the ante-natal ward, which shared an office with the consultant delivery unit.

'Whoops! Careful, Dr Rowan!' she exclaimed. 'Morning, Sister Pardoe—hi, Eve! Sorry I'm late. My alarm didn't go off. Are we still as busy as we were yesterday?'

Before anybody could reply, a weary-looking Nurse Kelsey appeared at the door.

'Can somebody give me a hand with the stretcher trolley?' she asked. 'There's not an auxiliary to be seen.'

'No problem,' said David Rowan promptly, and went off with Nurse Kelsey, the Handley pump under his arm as he manoeuvred the trolley along the corridor to the lifts.

'Extraordinary man, but the best registrar Mr Horsfield's ever had,' commented Sister Pardoe. Turning to Eve, she said kindly, 'Right, Sister, give us your report on your night's activities, and then get away to that nice, quiet flat of yours for a good sleep.'

When Eve had finally completed her writing and had left the hospital, the two day sisters exchanged remarks about her.

'I wonder just how much longer she and David Rowan are going to be so freezing towards each other,' mused Fay Mitchell. 'It's so embarrassing! They're both so competent, and you'd think they'd decide to bury it. I suppose they're both too proud to climb down.'

'Or too hurt,' remarked Sister Pardoe shrewdly. 'That can make folk very unforgiving sometimes.'

'But it was all so brief!' protested Fay.

'All the more humiliating for them,' observed the older midwife with a sigh.

'Oh, heavens, just *think* of it!' exclaimed Fay. 'Mustn't it have been *awful* when Philip opened the door and——?'

'Sssh!' warned Sister Pardoe as two ward domestics passed the office door. 'We'd better get ready for Mr Horsfield's round. Have we got all the scan reports and path. lab. results back?'

'Yes, I think I'm ready for the great man,' smiled Fay. 'And we'll meet the new junior obstetric houseman—Dr Spriggs. Wonder if he's nice—and single!'

'We've got to work with him for the next six months, whether he's nice or otherwise,' declared Sister Pardoe. 'As long as he does his job well, I'll leave the flirting to you young ones!'

'The poor man doesn't know what he's in for, does he?' laughed Fay.

'*Who* doesn't?' asked a well-bred female voice as Dr Lucinda Hallcross-Spriggs strolled into the office to introduce herself.

'There's a patient just delivered in Delivery Two, and another nearly fully dilated in Stage One A,' Sister Pardoe informed the night staff. 'I've told young Digweed that he can have the delivery, if that's all right with you, Sister West.'

'Fine, though I hope there'll be another some time during the night for Nurse Kelsey. It's her last night on,' replied Eve, exchanging a smile with the red-haired student midwife beside her.

'You'll probably get a few admissions; there are plenty due for March,' said the Scotswoman, getting up from the desk to go off duty. 'I won't wish you a quiet night, then, but, if you admit any, make sure you deliver them before eight a.m.!'

She wrapped her cloak around her, and as she left the office Miss O'Casey bustled in.

'Good evenin' to ye! Have ye seen there's a new admission just arrived? One o' those poor Asian ladies, God pity her. You know they never phone in to say they're comin'. There's a husband wid her, him wid a big turban on his head like the Sultan of Kashmir, and a mother-in-law wid a face on her that'd turn milk sour.'

'Good, that'll be a patient for you to deliver, Pat,' said Eve.

'I want to have a talk wid ye first, Nurse Kelsey,' interposed the nursing officer. 'I've got to do an assessment on ye, and send in a report—don't worry, it'll be quite a good one,' she added as the girl's face fell. 'Let me see, who else have we got on tonight? Sister Hicks on Post-Natal—God forgive me, but I hope they'll keep her busy enough to stay out o' the office; I can't be doin' wid all her talkin'——'

But at that moment Doris Hicks entered, all smiles.

'Do you know who I've just seen going out together?' she asked, her face alight with the pleasure of imparting news. 'Dr Philip Cranstone and Staff Nurse Gardner! They were just driving out as I cycled in. They didn't see me, and no wonder! They only had eyes for each other. Mark my words, we'll be hearing——'

'We'll be hearin' more than enough, Sister Hicks! Away wid ye and admit the new lady who's just come in. Her name's Mrs Hamadh, and ye can gossip all ye like to her, because she can't speak English. Sister West, ye'd better go and see what Dr Digweed is doin' wid' the patient in Stage One A, and I'll take Nurse Kelsey for a question-and-answer session in me own office downstairs. Off ye go!'

Eve was thankful to be spared any more gossip from Doris for the time being, and went to find the medical student, who was caring for a cheerful housewife in labour with her third child. Selwyn was now much more confident about his obstetric ability, and took it as a compliment that the midwives affectionately called him Dr Digweed.

'Everything is progressing satisfactorily with this lady, Sister, and I think we may predict a normal delivery.'

Eve smiled at the patient, who was bracing herself for the next contraction.

'Is your husband around, my dear?' Eve enquired.

'No fear! He's at home with our other two. I wouldn't like him to see me like this—we're not exactly at our best at these times, are we, Sister?' gasped the pleasant-faced woman as the pain subsided. Eve thought again how different couples were. Most patients liked to have their husbands or partners with them during the birth these days, but there were those who still considered it a woman's province, and did not want their menfolk to witness it. Eve believed firmly that all couples should be allowed to make their own choice, unpressured by the fads and fashions of the day.

Selwyn's forecast was proved correct, and before ten p.m. a healthy baby girl had been delivered, to her mother's joy: her other two children were boys.

'Nice work, Selwyn,' approved Eve as they examined the placenta. 'Let's ask Nancy to brew up for us all now, and then I'll wash her and you can start the paperwork.'

Selwyn was triumphant as he marched into the office, just as Nancy brought in a tray of tea and coffee.

'Thanks, Nancy! Take a cup to the new mother, will you?' asked Eve.

'And pour out another two, Nancy, please.'

They looked up at hearing Dr Rowan's voice; his broad shoulders filled the doorway, and behind him stood a tall, fine-featured young woman who stared appraisingly at the blonde beauty of Eve West.

'Good evening, ladies,' said David with a quick glance towards Eve. 'I've brought our new obstetric house officer to meet you all—Dr Lucinda Hallcross-Spriggs, to be known as just Dr Spriggs while on duty. Lucy, this is Sister West, one of the senior midwives on night duty here.'

Eve rose from the desk and held out her hand to the new junior doctor.

'Hi,' said the young woman casually and, turning to Rowan, she gave a rippling laugh.

'I say, David, you really have got some very attractive midwives at Beltonshaw!' she declared. 'What with Sister Mitchell on day duty, and now Sister West—oh *my*!'

She spoke with the total unselfconsciousness of an upper-class English girl used to being admired and indulged. Dr Rowan looked slightly embarrassed, and Eve treated Dr Spriggs to a long, cool grey-green stare as she resumed her seat. The awkward silence was broken by Miss O'Casey's entering the office.

'That's right handsomely spoken, Dr Spriggs, but, seein' that ye're here to deliver babies and not to re-stock a harem, I don't see how the looks o' the midwives have much bearin' on the matter!'

Pat Kelsey, who had followed the bright-eyed little Irishwoman into the office, suppressed a giggle. David Rowan spoke quickly.

'Ah, Miss O'Casey, good evening to you. I'm just introducing Dr Spriggs to the night staff.'

'So I see, Dr Rowan. Well, I hope ye'll enjoy your six months with us, Dr Spriggs, and we'll treat ye as well as ye treat us.'

'Good evening, how do you do, Miss O'Casey?' said the young woman doctor, somewhat taken aback by such directness.

While the others chatted, Eve looked straight at David with stony composure as she reported on the situation in the delivery unit.

'There's a multigravida just delivered, and another patient in labour, Mrs Tahmina Hamadh. Sister Hicks is admitting her,' she informed him. 'Her English is very limited, and her husband has to act as interpreter. It's her second baby. Sister Hicks will give you the details.'

'Thank you, Sister.' He nodded with formal politeness, and, turning to Nancy, he smiled and accepted a cup of coffee. 'Cheers, Nancy!'

Sister Doris Hicks hurried into the office.

'Mrs Hamadh isn't doing very much yet,' she announced. 'I've left her on the monitor for a bit. Her husband and mother-in-law are with her, to make sure she isn't left alone with a male doctor! Oh, good evening, Dr Rowan—have you brought our new houseman—er—house officer to meet us?'

'Yes, indeed I have, Sister Hicks. This is Dr Lucinda Hallcross-Spriggs,' he said, knowing that the older midwife would be impressed.

'Hallcross-Spriggs? Oh, my goodness! Are you related to the Member of Parliament?' asked Doris eagerly.

'I'm his daughter, actually,' replied the young woman with a smile.

'His *daughter*? Oh, how marvellous!' cried the sister. 'Just wait till I tell my youngsters that I'm working with the daughter of Sir Peter Hallcross-Spriggs! Mr Horsfield must be thrilled to have you on his team!'

She looked round at her colleagues, rather surprised that nobody seemed to be sharing her enthusiasm. Eve was writing the midnight totals of patients admitted, delivered and discharged from the delivery unit in the last twenty-four hours, and did not look up, though she now remembered where she had heard the new doctor's name. Dr Spriggs's father was a baronet and MP, in line for a ministerial post in the next Cabinet reshuffle.

'Yes, Daddy's pleased that I'm working under Mr Horsfield, and wants to sound him out about the maternity services in the north-west,' she told Sister Hicks. 'I must say, I'm very impressed with everything so far!'

'Do you live in London, Doctor?' asked Doris.

'No, Hallcross Park's in Wiltshire, but Daddy has a flat in London, which is useful, of course. I lived in London during my training at St Margaret's—that was tremendous fun!'

'Just fancy!' enthused Doris admiringly. 'You could have been a débutante and had a wonderful time going to balls and parties and having your picture in the society columns. And yet you chose to train as a doctor!'

'Oh, I'd have *loathed* being a débutante!' laughed Lucinda. 'Taking a medical degree was far more amusing!'

She turned a dazzling smile upon David, who put down his empty cup and turned to leave the office.

'Thank you for the coffee, Nancy, and—er—everybody. Dr Spriggs will be on call tonight, but if you're worried about anything, Sister West, don't hesitate to give me a buzz, and I'll come over as well. Goodnight!'

'Goodnight, ladies,' said Dr Spriggs, adding, 'Perhaps we shall meet again before morning!'

The two white-coated figures strolled away down the corridor.

'I just can't believe this!' exclaimed Doris Hicks. 'The Honourable Lucinda Hallcross-Spriggs!'

'Ye'll be curtsyin' to her next, me dear,' chuckled Miss O'Casey. 'Whether she's a princess or a dustman's daughter, it's as a *doctor* we're goin' to know her. I'll reserve judgement for a week or two, before gettin' over-friendly too soon.'

'Personally I think she's going to be insufferable,' muttered Eve.

'Now, now, Sister, don't go to the other extreme,'

warned the nursing officer. 'She can't help the way she talks, any more than I can!'

Amid the ensuing laughter, Nancy added with a wink, 'I'll tell you something, I think she's got her eye on Dr Rowan already!'

Eve's mouth tightened as she completed the midnight returns form.

'Heavens, it's twelve o'clock,' said Miss O'Casey. 'Come on, Sister West, ye took tired out—tuck yeself up on the sofa in the rest-room for an hour, and have a little nap. Sister Hicks and Nurse Kelsey, you stay here on the delivery unit till one, and keep an eye on Mrs Hamadh. I'll go down to Post-Natal and see how they're doin'.'

'Thank you, I'll go to the rest-room, then,' said Eve, handing over her keys to Sister Hicks. As she went out of the office she nearly bumped into Mr Hamadh, who presented himself at the door.

'My wife is having great pain now. She needs a woman to help her,' he said sternly.

Sister Hicks and Pat Kelsey rose immediately, and found Tahmina Hamadh writhing on her bed, uttering little birdlike cries of pain as each new contraction seized her.

Wrapped in the warm scarlet-lined cloak that had been hers for seven years, Eve tried to settle herself for a nap, but her restless thoughts would not allow her even to doze. The encounter with the new young woman doctor had disturbed her; it was bad enough to endure the icy barrier between herself and David Rowan, without having to watch another attractive woman making a play for him. For the hundredth time she asked herself why— oh, *why* had she behaved so foolishly, so indiscreetly?

And there was no way that she could turn the clock back now.

Andrew Rayner had been pressing her to go out with him lately, and so far she had refused, not having the heart for any sort of social life while she was still smarting under her terrible humiliation. But now she began to wonder if an evening out would do her good; Andrew chose the very best restaurants, and it would be nice to dress herself really smartly and get away from the hospital atmosphere for an evening. She made up her mind to accept Andrew's invitation next time he mentioned it.

At one o'clock she returned to the delivery unit, where she found an argument going on between Sister Hicks and Mr Hamadh.

'I do not want for any man to examine my wife, only woman!' he was saying emphatically.

'That will depend on whether or not your wife needs a doctor,' retorted Sister Hicks. 'All of the midwives are women, but the only woman doctor we have is very junior, with not much experience. We may have to call for Dr Rowan, who's very good at his job——'

'*No man!*' insisted Mr Hamadh loudly. 'In my country we have no need of men to help our wives with childbearing, only women!'

'If we need to call Dr Rowan to see your wife we shall do so, whether you like it or not!' replied Doris Hicks in exasperation, and Eve stepped forward, putting on her most winning professional smile.

'All right, Sister Hicks, you go back to Post-Natal now, and I'll deal with Mrs Hamadh,' she said with quiet authority. Turning to the turbanned and bearded man, she spoke reassuringly.

'If your wife makes good progress in labour, Mr Hamadh, the chances are that she won't need a doctor at all,' she told him. 'We shall take very great care of her, I promise you. However, if she needs a doctor for her own safety—or your baby's safety—we shall call for one, and you will understand, I'm sure. You may stay with her all the time. You don't want your wife and child to be denied the best possible care, do you, Mr Hamadh?'

He looked surly, but Eve's persuasive common sense had its effect.

'If a man comes to her, I shall stay in the room,' he declared.

'Yes, I've just said so. Let's wait and see how Tahmina gets on, shall we? I'll examine her now.'

'If she does not have the child by morning, I will take her home,' he threatened.

'Oh, I'm sure you wouldn't do anything so foolish,' smiled Eve. 'Now, if you will go to the top of the bed and hold Tahmina's hand, I will examine her as gently as I can. Will you tell her that, please?'

The frightened woman watched them with soft dark eyes full of apprehension.

'Well done, Tahmina! You are in good labour now,' smiled Eve at the conclusion of the examination, and speaking in as simple terms as she could. 'I will give you an injection to ease the pain, and in a little while you will have your baby. Do you understand me, Tahmina?'

'That is good,' Mr Hamadh answered for his wife. 'You give her an injection, and I and my mother will stay beside her and wait for the baby.'

'All right, but please do not talk to her,' advised Eve. 'The injection will make her feel sleepy, and she needs to rest between the pains.'

Back in the office she checked the ampoule of meptid one hundred milligrams with Miss O'Casey.

'God knows it's a lonely life for some of these poor

Asian women,' commented the Irishwoman. 'They've left behind the culture they grew up in, to come to a strange place wid people speakin' a strange tongue.'

'And her children will grow up learning to speak English and learn Western ways that will cut them off from her,' added Eve.

'And would ye fancy bein' married to Mr Hamadh, Sister?' asked Miss O'Casey with a sly smile. 'It makes me count me single blessin's!'

An hour and a half went by, and Mrs Hamadh progressed to full dilatation of the cervix at a quarter to three; she was moved to the delivery room, and Nurse Kelsey checked the trolley with the delivery equipment and the resuscitation cot for the baby. Eve got ready to supervise the student midwife, while Miss O'Casey hovered discreetly in the background, talking to the senior Mrs Hamadh, a formidable lady who was quite bewildered by Western methods of giving birth.

'I think we're having a little trouble here,' whispered Eve, indicating the monitor, which showed some marked deceleration of the baby's heartbeat.

'Hm,' muttered the nursing officer with a frown at the tracing. 'Can ye see the head advancin'?'

'Not much. We *could* need a lift-out with forceps to speed things up a bit,' replied Eve in a low tone.

'I'll go and bleep Dr Spriggs, and I'd better bleep Dr Rowan as well, seein' as it's only her first night on,' decided Miss O'Casey.

The two doctors arrived together, Lucinda bright and excited. Miss O'Casey explained Mr Hamadh's aversion to the thought of a man attending his wife, so David tactfully stayed outside the delivery room, relying on the observations of the midwives and Dr Spriggs to let him know if a forceps delivery would be needed.

The baby's head began to advance well, but the dips in the heart-rate continued. Eve was not happy.

'I think we'll need Dr Rowan to come and do a low forceps to get this baby out as soon as possible,' she said to Dr Spriggs. 'Will you pass me Wrigley's forceps from the shelf over there, and I'll prepare the trolley for him?'

David Rowan entered the room and smiled at the patient and her husband.

'Good morning! I'm Dr Rowan, and, as your baby seems to be getting a little bit tired, I'm going to help it to be born very soon. Will somebody please bleep the paediatrician on call? It's Dr Linda Stalley. We'd better have her standing by.'

Mr Hamadh stood at his wife's side as if rooted to the floor. He found that he was grateful to the competent and authoritative man who had come to help his wife. The baby's dark head was now visible with each contraction.

'Just one moment, Dr Rowan!' Eve suddenly interrupted. 'The head's coming up very quickly now, and I think that if I perform an episiotomy we'll be able to deliver the baby normally with the next contraction.'

She turned to the patient. 'Tahmina, I'm just going to make a little cut down here, so that your baby's head can come through easily and safely. Is that all right?'

'Yes, yes, woman, do what you have to do!' cried Mr Hamadh impatiently.

And so at just after three-fifteen Nurse Kelsey had the joy of delivering a dark, wriggling little boy into the world, to be handed straight to the arms of his happy parents.

Eve West gave David Rowan a brief, brilliantly triumphant glance, which he acknowledged with a nod and a raised thumb. Dr Linda Stalley arrived to be greeted by a healthy yell of welcome from the newcomer.

'Sorry you've had a wasted journey, Doctor,' smiled Miss O'Casey, 'but ye can stay for a cup o' tea now ye're here. We'll soon be ready for a brew-up all round.'

When the third stage was completed, Dr Spriggs sat down on the surgeon's stool to start suturing the episiotomy, assisted by Nurse Kelsey; the rest of the staff adjourned to the office. Miss O'Casey chatted with Dr Stalley, who innocently remarked that she had met Philip Cranstone at a seminar on child abuse.

'He was looking very fit and happy,' she said. 'It seems that he's about to announce his engagement to that pretty little staff midwife, Annette Gardner—an excellent choice. She's just the right sort of girl for him.'

'Praise be to God,' breathed Miss O'Casey with such relief that David and Eve could not mistake her meaning, though they both appeared to be concentrating hard on their paperwork. When Dr Stalley took her leave, Miss O'Casey accompanied her down the corridor, leaving them alone in the office.

Eve finished writing out the three different birth notifications, and the entry in the heavy register of births, while Rowan completed his comments in Mrs Hamadh's case-notes. As she rose from her chair he drew a deep breath and, without looking up, he commented lightly on the delivery.

'Quite a difficult situation, wasn't it? Another case of cord compression, presumably. I'm very pleased that Nurse Kelsey got the delivery in the end.'

There was no reply, and he glanced up questioningly, only to find that he was alone and talking to himself. He shrugged. She was obviously not willing to respond to even the mildest friendly exchange, and he felt that he could hardly blame her.

In actual fact, Eve had quietly left the office before he had begun to speak, because she could not endure the unfriendly silence.

CHAPTER SIX

A ROW of wet mackintoshes hung in the staff cloakroom, where Sister Hicks, Staff Nurse Gardner and student midwife Nurse Barbara Gunn were preparing to go on duty.

'Is Miss O'Casey in charge tonight?' asked Nurse Gunn, a stocky, blunt-featured girl in her mid-twenties.

'No, Sister West is,' replied Doris Hicks, wiping the rain from her face; she was drenched to the skin after cycling through the downpour. 'Her car must be out of action, because she's just been driven in by a very large man! I saw her getting out of his car at the back entrance.'

'Oho! Has she found another one already?' grinned Nancy, who had just come in with squelching shoes and a dripping umbrella. 'Perhaps it's that sales rep. who lives in the flat below hers. He takes her out to dinner sometimes, and you can bet he gets invited in afterwards for coffee and all the et ceteras!'

Annette turned round sharply.

'That remark was quite uncalled-for, Nancy,' she said with a rebuke that caused the others to stare in surprise. 'Sister West is an excellent midwife, and that's all that need concern us. Her private life is her own business.'

Nancy's mouth dropped open, and Doris Hicks decided on a quick change of subject.

'Dr Hallcross-Spriggs is on call—I heard that delicious laugh of hers as I came up the stairs. Isn't she attractive?'

'Oh, yes, you can hear the Lady Lucinda's high-class giggle everywhere you go,' sniffed Barbara. 'I suppose we'll have to hear all about Daddy's big speech in the Commons, and what he said to the Prime Minister over tea!'

'Can't you just imagine the sort of life she's had?' commented Nancy, recovering from Annette's snub. 'Doting parents and nanny, private schools and everything—you can tell she's been spoilt rotten by the way she likes to get her own way, but she's certainly a charmer!'

'I'm not so keen on the way she orders us around like servants,' objected Barbara in her downright Lancashire tones. 'She said to me, "Do up my gown at the back, will you?" I said to her, "*I* was always taught to say please!"'

'Come on, it's time we were on duty,' Annette reminded them. There was a new confidence about Staff Nurse Gardner that reflected the light in her eyes and the spring in her step. She was a girl in love, and knew herself to be loved in return. She held no malice in her heart which was so full of happiness.

It was common knowledge that Lucinda Hallcross-Spriggs was attracted to Dr Rowan. Her bright, intelligent eyes would seek his glance, and her uninhibited peals of laughter brought a smile to his rather sombre features. Her tall, willowy figure looked good even in the green theatre gear that hid her masses of dark hair. As a member of the obstetric team, working alongside Rowan in the wards, theatre and delivery rooms, discussing patients' problems in the ante-natal clinic and sharing the doctors' mess and common-room, she had every opportunity to charm him into falling in love with her.

Eve had to stand by and see it happening, and she kept outwardly calm, though inwardly she suffered. It was no consolation to know that she was responsible for David's attitude towards her as she now watched him being drawn to another woman, one who was rich and attractive and shared his profession, as well as having a prestigious family background. Eve's own parents were divorced, and both had remarried. Her only sister was married, and had a noisy, undisciplined family, and the aunt who had shown Eve love and understanding was dead, leaving her the money that had bought the flat, the car and the means to pursue her chosen career in comfort. Eve enjoyed her work, and took a pride in doing it to the best of her ability, but she knew that she was not like Miss O'Casey, for whom worthwhile work and independence could be a satisfying substitute for marriage and mother-hood. For most women, a loving relationship with a man was essential to happiness, and Eve was no exception. She gave a sigh as she walked into the office and greeted Sister Pardoe who was ready to go off duty.

At eleven o'clock that night the atmosphere in the office appeared to be relaxed and cheerful as the staff discussed their patients over coffee and a home-made cake brought in by Sister Hicks.

'So Mrs Thompson's for induction of labour tomorrow. Keep an eye on her blood-pressure, won't you?' warned Dr Spriggs infuriatingly. 'My word, Sister Hicks, this cake's extremely good! I simply must have another slice, even if it *is* bad for the figure. Aren't you going to have another slice, Sister West?'

Eve did not reply, and Lucinda looked hard at her.

'Is everything all right, Sister? You look awfully pale, and your eyes are positively cavernous!'

Eve took a sip of strong coffee. Sister Hicks might find Lucinda's openness disarming, but it only got on Eve's nerves.

There was certainly nothing underhand about

Lucinda's approach to David Rowan, who came in at that moment.

'Hi, David, I've heard from the parents today,' she told him. 'Daddy's invited Mr and Mrs Horsfield to a weekend house-party at Easter, just at the beginning of your week's holiday. Mummy's dying to meet this dedicated surgeon who gave up a great career in Johannesburg because he disagreed with the political set-up! So I do hope that you can come, too. Mr Horsfield would be glad to have you there to back him up in his chats with Daddy.'

'Oh, I don't think so, Lucy,' he said awkwardly. 'I'm studying hard for the fellowship exams, and besides, I'm not much good at parties.'

'What rot! I'll phone Mummy tomorrow and tell her that you're coming. The break will do you good!'

Significant looks were exchanged between the staff, though Rowan muttered something about having to wait and see, while giving Lucinda an indulgent smile as if she were a pert little girl of about twelve.

Eve got up from the desk and went to find something— anything—to do in the empty stage one and delivery rooms. She could not endure another moment of Lucinda's chatter. Alone in Stage One Room A, she closed her eyes and put her hand to her forehead as tears welled up and spilled over. Tearing a square of paper towel from the roll on the wall-bracket, she carefully wiped them away before proceeding to check and replenish the shelves with intravenous fluids, syringes and needles, examination gloves and all the equipment ready for use. Finally she checked her reflection in the wall-mirror. No smudges! It was safe to return, and thankfully the doctors had left.

Midwifery tended to be all or nothing. The delivery

unit was either hectically busy or boringly quiet, and some midwives believed that there was a connection with phases of the moon. At three a.m. Eve was stifling a yawn and Sister Hicks's head was nodding over her knitting. . .but they sat up sharply as a call-bell rang from the ante-natal ward.

It was Mrs Janet Thompson, who was for induction the next day: nature had intervened.

'I've been getting backache ever since eleven o'clock, Sister,' she told Eve. 'And now my tummy is tightening up every five or six minutes. Do you think I might be starting in labour?'

She broke off and grimaced as another contraction began, and Eve placed a hand lightly on the tensely hardened muscles that were preparing for the birth of her first baby.

'I think you are, love. Well done!' Eve reassured her, and led her to Stage One Room A, where she applied the external monitor.

'Oh, I'm so pleased, Sister! It must have been the thought of that induction that's got me going!' exclaimed Janet delightedly.

Eve put Nurse Gunn in charge of her, and wondered if she would be delivered before the night shift ended; Eve was glad of some action to take her mind off her brooding thoughts.

Unfortunately there was always a possibility of a sudden obstetric emergency, and Eve's reflections were interrupted when Barbara called to her in a low, urgent tone.

'Could you come, Sister? She's losing blood, more than just the usual "show", I think.'

Eve agreed with her. Any abnormal haemorrhage needed a doctor's immediate attention, and Eve phoned at once for Dr Spriggs, who appeared within minutes, a white coat thrown over blue pyjamas.

'Blood-pressure a hundred and fifty over ninety-five—the baby's heart-rate is normal, as you can see,' said Eve, pointing to the monitor. 'The blood loss is only slight, but it's persistent. If it's a placental abruption, we're in trouble,' she added in a very low whisper.

'I'll do a gentle internal examination,' said Lucinda. 'Fetch me a pair of size seven gloves and a speculum, will you?'

'Actually you'd be wiser to phone Dr Rowan and ask *him* to come over and examine her,' said Eve firmly, and for a moment their eyes met in opposition. Dr Spriggs hesitated, then bit her lip and finally nodded, realising that she was not being obstructed in her work by a bossy midwife, but was being offered a tactful face-saver. She also realised that Eve would telephone Dr Rowan if she did not.

'Perhaps you're right, Sister West. I'd better let David know.'

Her well-bred accent and rippling laugh could be heard in the office.

'Hi, David, it's me. Sorry! Yes, three-twenty a.m.! Oh, that's very sweet of you! Look, I've got this woman in early labour, first baby, was down for induction tomorrow—blood-pressure a bit high—well, she's losing rather more than the usual "show", I feel. Could you possibly come over and see what you think of her? No, I haven't examined her because I thought it might be wiser to leave that to you. Sure. Yes, of course, David, I'll tell them. Thanks awfully. See you!'

'Dr Rowan will be over straight away,' she called to Eve, adding unnecessarily, 'You'd better alert the

anaesthetist and paediatrician on call—we could be
having a Caesarean section!'

Eve was already checking the maternity threatre, and
Barbara was preparing to assist at taking blood samples
and commencing an intravenous drip. The tall figure of
David Rowan strode up the corridor, and by the time he
had decided to play safe and perform a Caesarean the
staff were almost ready to begin. Janet signed the form
of consent to an operation, and her husband was asked to
come to the hospital immediately.

Eve's heart pounded with the excitement she always
felt as she donned the white canvas shoes, green theatre
cap, gown and face-mask, and finally the gloves. She
opened the Caesarean pack, and laid out the tools of her
profession in perfect order, a vital member of the life-
saving obstetric team.

Dr Rowan performed the operation, assisted by Dr
Spriggs and Sister West, with Dr Okoje from Uganda as
anaesthetist. A fine, healthy boy uttered his first cry at
four-fifteen, to the joy and thankfulness of his father,
who was anxiously waiting outside in the theatre annexe.
A large retro-placental blood-clot was discovered, and
two units of blood were rushed over from the laboratory
to replace the heavy loss that Janet had sustained.
Without the operation, both the lives of mother and baby
would have been lost.

Lucinda looked at Rowan above her mask as she
listened to him explaining each step of the procedure to
her, while Eve's anticipation of his every requirement
made for their usual smooth teamwork, though Eve felt
that her patience was being sorely tried.

'Haven't you got clips for the skin closure, Sister?' he
asked as he came to the final joining together of the
incision.

'No, black silk thread, Doctor,' she replied.

'Silk? You know I like Michel clips for the skin, Sister,' he frowned.

'I'm quite familiar with theatre routine, Doctor, but I'm thinking of the mother's comfort,' she replied coolly. 'Metal clips may be all right for horses—or for yourself if you ever have your appendix out——'

Lucinda giggled, and Dr Okoje's brown eyes twinkled. David looked at Eve with an expression that was hard to define.

'All right, Sister, we won't argue at this hour. Give me what you've got there.'

He took the threaded needle from her gloved hand, and allowed Lucinda to put in the stitches while he watched and commented. The operation completed, he pulled off his gloves and snatched the cap from his thick dark hair.

'Thank you, everybody! Get the kettle on, Nancy, I could murder a cup of coffee!'

Eve cleared her instrument trolley as Nancy and the theatre technician wheeled the sleeping Janet Thompson out of the theatre.

'Thank God that's over,' she murmured to herself.

And then there was the unexpected hand upon her shoulder, and the deep voice speaking hesitantly behind her.

'Thank you once again, Eve. You always do a superb job in Theatre. I'm sorry if I was a bit impatient, and you were quite right about the skin closure.'

She drew a sharp intake of breath, unable to take in what she was hearing. David Rowan had come back to thank her, to speak the first words of a personal nature since. . . She had to make a great effort to control herself, to stop herself from turning round and throwing her arms around his neck, weeping on his shoulder, sobbing out all her bitter regrets. . .

Instead she stood absolutely still.

'Er—are you all right, Eve?' he asked, keeping his hand on her shoulder. Its touch seemed to warm her whole body.

Slowly, hesitantly, she placed her own hand over his, and a wave of relief swept over her, so sweet that she almost thought she would faint and fall. Still she did not turn to face him.

'Oh, David, I never intended you any harm,' she whispered.

But then from outside the theatre she heard the sound of Lucinda's peals of girlish laughter in the office, and the word '*David*!' echoing along the corridor. Of course! It was his new-found interest and attraction to the young woman doctor which was making him call a truce and be friendly towards her again. It was Lucinda who was responsible for this thawing of the cold war—in just the same way that Annette Gardner, happy and secure in Philip's love, was now willing to forget the past.

Realising this, Eve tensed. What a fool she had nearly made of herself!

She removed her hand quickly from his, and muttered in a low voice harsh with suppressed emotion, 'All right, just leave me alone now, please.'

Sensing her sudden recoil, he attempted to take hold of her shoulders and gently turn her round to face him.

'My dear, I just wanted to apologise——'

She shrugged him off violently, and he stepped back.

'Eve! What's the matter?'

'For God's sake, leave me alone to get on with my work!'

'I see,' he said quietly. 'Very well, Sister.'

And he left her, returning to the office, where Lucinda handed him the longed-for cup of coffee.

Outside, the rain continued to pour down steadily from the night sky as Eve leaned over the operating table, her hands clenched. She knew that she should have accepted his honest offer of friendship, but she could not bear to be just friends with David Rowan as he fell more deeply in love with Lucinda. Her own obsession with him was too great—and she had to admit it—so was her pride.

The thought of Andrew Rayner came to her; he had driven her to work because she had found her car with a flat tyre. Might Andrew be a way to drive David Rowan from her heart?

CHAPTER SEVEN

IT WAS the Thursday before Easter, Eve's first night off after four nights on duty—and it had been a disaster, disagreeable enough to make her reconsider moving away from Beltonshaw. She had accepted an invitation to dine with Andrew Rayner in one of Manchester's most expensive restaurants, and it had been obvious from the start of the evening that he thought they were embarking on a much closer relationship. Eve had in fact toyed with the idea herself, but found it quite impossible to dispel the image of Rowan's face from her mind.

When she and Andrew had returned to Jubilee House shortly before midnight he had taken her in his arms on the landing outside the door of his flat.

'Your place or mine, Eve darling?' he'd smiled, confident in his anticipation of her surrender that night.

But she had drawn away from him, and with a most untypical agitation she had rushed up the stairs to the third floor.

'No, Andrew, I'm sorry, but I can't!' she had pleaded, fumbling in her handbag for her key.

He had chased after her with unexpected agility for an overweight man who had had a fair amount to drink.

'What the hell's the matter with you, Eve? Come on, you can't say you haven't given me good reason to expect——'

'I know, Andrew, and I'm sorry, but—please let me *go*!' she had demanded as he had grasped her shoulder and forced her body against his.

'Have I said something to upset you, or what?' he asked impatiently.

'No, not at all.'

'Then what's up?'

And out came the words Eve had never intended to say.

'There's someone else, Andrew. Another man.'

He laughed shortly. 'You could have fooled *me*! I haven't seen any other man here since I moved in, and I've watched pretty closely. May I ask who is this favoured individual—a doctor at the hospital?'

'Yes. Now, will you please go, Andrew? I'm tired.'

'I bet the bastard's married. Well, you're free to wreck your life in your own way. Goodnight, Eve, and thanks for nothing!'

She felt utterly depressed as she ran a bath and lay in the steaming, scented water before going to bed. As she settled under the duvet a ray of comfort came to her: at least she had avoided a serious false step—and, when she awoke on the morning of Good Friday, her first thought was the same. If she had allowed Andrew to come to bed with her she would always have regretted it.

Sadly her thoughts turned towards David Rowan, now weekending at Hallcross Park in the company of Lucinda and her parents, with Mr and Mrs Horsfield among the guests. Because of what had happened between them when he had been temporarily and disastrously bewitched by her for a few hours, she was now unable to share herself with any other man. And David, it seemed, was soon to belong to another woman.

The telephone rang, and Eve was pleased to hear the friendly voice of Fay Mitchell.

'Hello, Eve! I'm off for the day, and wondered if you were doing anything. Listen, I've got the most amazing

thing to tell you! It's too good for the phone—can we
meet for lunch or something?'

'Oh, come over and have lunch here—that would be
lovely!' Eve answered warmly, and when her colleague
arrived she was greeted with a hug that made Fay suspect
that her phone call had been well timed.

'How's your amorous neighbour?' she asked.

'Oh, we've fallen out, I'm afraid, Fay. The usual
story—he wanted it and I didn't.'

'Hard luck,' grinned Fay. 'That's the trouble with
platonic friendships, isn't it? They won't stay that way.
Especially when the girl's got your looks and—er——'

'Reputation? Quite,' replied Eve drily.

'Now I didn't say that,' protested Fay. 'It's just that
you've got a sort of built-in attraction for men that drives
them all crazy.'

'Not quite all of them,' corrected Eve. 'I can think of
one notable exception at least.'

'Ah, yes, well, David Rowan's a law unto himself,'
said Fay. 'A lot of us think that he treated you pretty
badly, Fay—after all, it takes two. Anyway, he's going
to have some explaining to do at Hallcross Park this
weekend, by the sound of things! Are we sitting comfortably? Then I'll begin. . .'

Eve was grateful for Fay's high spirits, and smiled
indulgently at her impish little face as they settled
together on the settee. But soon Eve was sitting bolt
upright in surprise as Fay's story proceeded.

'Yesterday morning—Thursday—Mr Horsfield came
in to review the ante-natal patients and see if any could
be sent home for Easter, before he himself went away,
and Dr Rowan too—you know that Mr Andreasson's
coming back to do a locum job while Rowan's on holiday.
So off we all trailed round the ward in the usual reverent

hush while the great man peered at each patient over the top of his half-moons. . .and we came to this new patient, Dawn Totman, a Londoner who's come to live up north to be near her boyfriend. She's older than the usual single mums we get—in her early thirties—and not due for another six weeks, but she'll have to stay in because the scan shows a low-lying placenta, right down to the cervix. She could start bleeding at any time, and need an emergency Caesarean. Anyway, she's a real cheeky madam with the broadest Cockney accent you ever heard. When Mr Horsfield said, "Good morning, Mrs Totman,"—she calls herself Mrs—she said, "Same to you, Guv'nor!"—and then she looked straight past him and said, "Well, if it ain't Dave Rowan! Fancy meeting up wiv *you* after all these years!"'

Fay was a good mimic, and Eve gasped at hearing the repeated words.

'Who was she? A former patient?'

'No, Eve, she remembered him from way back to childhood. "Ain't you done well, Dave?" she said. "Don't say you've gorn and forgot your little friend Dawn from next door!"'

'A *Londoner* you said? She must have made a mistake,' said Eve.

'Evidently not, because she went on to say, "Don't pretend you've forgotten me, Dave, or I'll fink you've forgotten your *own* family as well! We was neighbours in the old Beck's Cross Road, you and me, and sat togevver at the same desk at Beck's Cross Junior!"'

'How did he take it?' asked Eve in astonishment.

'Well, Mr Horsfield cut in and told her she'd have to sort out her connection with Dr Rowan later—and then Sister Pardoe smiled and said that Dr Rowan had come from South Africa, at which Dawn shook her head.

"Don't you believe 'im, Sister, 'e's an East-Ender, same as me!" Then Dr Spriggs had to join in; you know she can never keep *her* mouth shut, even in front of Mr Horsfield. She said, "Just ignore the woman, David." It was meant to be in an undertone, but that Oxford accent of hers carries for yards, and Dawn Totman really flared up. "You'd better not try ignoring *me*, Dave," she told him, "not like you ignore your poor Mum, who done 'er best for you. *You* may 'ave lost your memory, but *I* 'aven't, and I don't think much of people who forget their families and old friends when they've gorn up in the world!"'

'How awful!' gasped Eve. 'Fay, you're not making this up, are you? I mean, you're not exaggerating, or anything?'

'Guide's honour,' insisted Fay. 'She's going to be in Ante-Natal for the next few weeks, so you'll meet her yourself. She amuses the other patients with her Cockney accent, and she's not going to go away—or stop talking!'

'But everybody knows that Dr Rowan came over from Johannesburg,' protested Eve. 'You've only got to hear his accent—and all the things he has to say about obstetrics out there, in hospitals and bush clinics.'

'But when you come to think about it, Eve, his accent isn't all *that* pronounced, is it? Haven't you noticed sometimes, at a critical moment in the delivery room or theatre, his accent does take on a bit of a London twang—as if he'd forgotten to keep up the South African clip, and his natural way of talking had slipped out unawares?'

'Now that you mention it, I have noticed,' said Eve slowly, remembering when he had spoken to her in scorn and anger. Her face clouded. 'But Fay, this woman *must* be mistaking him for someone else!'

Fay shook her head. 'I'm not so sure,' she said. 'He didn't actually deny it, in fact he hardly said anything at all, but he looked quite pale. You know, Eve, he's never said anything about parents or family in South Africa. He's never talked about his background, only his work experience. I'm telling you, Dawn was pretty convincing, and we're going to hear a lot more from her—there are no secrets at Beltonshaw General! Oh, Eve, I'm sorry, love, I didn't mean——'

'It's all right, Fay, everybody knows about "Rowan and West",' replied Eve with a tightening of her lips.

'Yes, and they also know that you're still here, still one of our best midwives, and the fairest of us all!' rejoined Fay loyally. 'There were plenty who thought that you'd leave Beltonshaw after that little episode, but they were mistaken. We all admired the dignified way you kept going and faced all the——' She hesitated.

'Humiliation is the word you're looking for, Fay,' prompted Eve with a bitter little smile.

'Oh, my dear. . .well, Rowan had no right to turn against you in the way that he did, but it looks as if he's going to get his come-uppance from this Totman woman. It'll certainly rub some of the bloom off his weekend at Hallcross Park, and it'll be interesting to hear what Lucinda makes of these revelations of a London East-End background!'

'If it's true, which I can't believe,' returned Eve.

They continued to discuss the mystery over a leisurely lunch of pizza and salad, and then watched a film on television about the events of the first Good Friday.

After she had driven Fay back to Beltonshaw and deposited her at the nurses' home, Eve slipped into the hospital chapel for a few minutes. There had been a service for patients and staff there earlier in the day, and the place was silent and peaceful as Eve sat with her golden head bowed. She was not a regular churchgoer, but she found herself saying a short prayer for the man she loved as he faced a possible threat to his position and prestige among his colleagues.

Then she sighed with thankfulness that she had not yielded to Andrew Rayner. . .

When Eve returned to duty on the night of Easter Sunday, Sister Pardoe had just supervised two normal deliveries within minutes of each other; one had been conducted by a medical student, one by a student midwife. Eve's first task was to transfer the new mothers and their babies to the post-natal ward downstairs, and clear away the trolleys and soiled linen.

'You get on with your writing-up, Sister Pardoe. Nancy and I will soon shift this lot!' she said briskly as the Scotswoman and the two trainees faced the usual formidable pile of paperwork that followed every delivery: the case-notes of the mothers and babies, the three different birth notification forms, the record of all medication given, including separate charts for intravenous fluids and yet another form for epidural anaesthetics, the number of which was constantly increasing; finally the details had to be entered in the weighty register of births. Sister Pardoe was twenty minutes late going off duty, by which time Eve and the auxiliary had cleaned and replenished the delivery rooms and stage one rooms, which were now ready to receive their next occupants.

Sister Doris Hicks was rushing distractedly to and fro in the ante-natal ward, where three patients were on complete bed-rest and needed hourly recordings of their blood-pressure; one of them had an intravenous drip in progress to supply her with a carefully measured amount of the drug ritodrine to try to avert premature labour.

The diabetic patient Mrs Joyce Graham had been re-admitted to have samples of her blood taken every four hours to assess the sugar levels over a twenty-four-hour period.

'Shall I do the ten o'clock blood-pressures for you, and take the diabetic's blood specimen?' Eve offered. 'You can get on with your medicine round, and Nancy can do the night drinks at the same time.'

'Oh, thank you, Eve. I've got Mr Andreasson coming up soon to see the woman with acute pyelonephritis, and he's sure to put her on intravenous antibiotics,' sighed Doris, who was not particularly well organised when faced with a busy ward.

''Ere, let me give an 'and with them drinks, Nancy,' said a bold Cockney voice near by. 'You pour 'em out, and I'll take 'em round. We'll soon get 'em done togevver!'

Eve felt a shiver of hostility as she realised that the blowsy woman in the purple nylon housecoat must be Dawn Totman.

'Sugar, dear?' enquired Dawn as she approached the patient whose blood-pressure Eve was recording. 'Oooh, I 'aven't come across *this* sister before—jeepers! The midwives up north are a jolly sight better-looking than the lot down at Beck's Cross! No wonder that a certain old acquaintance of mine came up 'ere to do 'is doctoring! What's your name, Blondie?'

'I'm Sister West, and I presume that you are Mrs Totman,' replied Eve coolly, her eyes intent on the falling column of mercury.

'Oooh, I've made a name for myself already in 'ere, by the sound of it!' sniggered Dawn. 'Are you on for the night, Sister?'

'Yes, but I work in the delivery unit, so you won't be

seeing much of me,' answered Eve, determined not to be
over-familiar with this woman. Some of the staff and
patients found her amusing, but after Fay Mitchell's
warning Eve felt threatened by her. She said as much in
the office later when she and Doris were having a quick
cup of coffee.

'Oh, I don't think there's any real harm in her,' said
Doris. 'At least she makes the other ante-natal mums
laugh and forget about their own problems for a while.'

'Maybe, but she's spreading the most awful stories
about Dr Rowan's family—if it really *is* his family,'
interposed Nancy with a dubious shake of her head. 'She
says they were notorious, the father drank and the mother
owed money everywhere. She says that David was the
one bright member of the family, but that none of the
others are up to much. His brother is a builder's labourer,
a right layabout, she says, and——'

'That's quite enough o' that, thank ye, Nancy. Sure
and she doesn't need your assistance in belittlin' Dr
Rowan's people,' came the sharp rebuke of Miss
O'Casey, who had tip-tapped quietly along the corridor
and now entered the office. 'If only half o' what she says
is true, the doctor will have enough embarrassment to
face when he comes back from his holiday, God help
him, and if it's *not* true it'll be up to him to decide what
to do about it. One thing's certain; it's his affair and not
ours. We're only concerned wid his work as an obstetrician, which is more than satisfactory. His family background is somethin' else. I advise ye all to be careful not
to repeat any gossip from Dawn Totman, or ye could
find yeselves in trouble!'

'But it's all over the ward, Miss O'Casey!' said Nancy.
'Every ante-natal patient knows that he was a precocious
child and used to get up at six o'clock in the morning to

practise on his mouth-organ for the school concert. It drove the Totmans crazy, she said.'

'Yes, and he was the only child at Beck's Cross Junior to win a scholarship to a boys' grammar school,' added Doris Hicks. 'She says he wore the most awful second-hand uniform, and the other boys called him Professor Pong because of his socks and pants when they had to strip off for the showers. Aren't children cruel?'

'Sure, they're nearly as cruel as grown-up people who ought to know better than to repeat such things!' exclaimed Miss O'Casey indignantly. 'God give me strength, Sister Hicks, will ye never learn? Away wid your idle gossip! And wasn't it all the more credit to the poor little feller, then, that he ended up as head boy o' that grammar school, and went on to university and medical trainin'? I got Dawn Totman to admit that much when I asked her if the David Rowan she knew had passed his O levels and A levels. She couldn't deny that his achievements had been outstandin'.'

'So do you think that he really is the same David Rowan, and didn't come from South Africa after all?' asked Nancy politely, with a quick glance at Eve and Doris.

'I'm inclined to think that he's probably who she says he is,' replied Miss O'Casey regretfully. 'He certainly came to *us* from South Africa, but he's never claimed to be born there. We only assumed it, and he's never corrected us, that's all. Why should he be obliged to tell us all about himself? His accent could be Australian, for all I know or care! Mr Horsfield will know about his place of birth, trainin' and so on—but, unlike *some* o' the members o' staff here, Mr Horsfield doesn't gossip like a fishwife!'

They were silent, and Eve felt grateful for Miss O'Casey's integrity and common sense.

'I think the woman's dangerous, and we should avoid any unnecessary conversation with her,' she volunteered.

'Maybe so, Sister West, but remember she's our *patient* first an' foremost, an' we're here to do our best for her, not sit in judgement,' the Irishwoman pointed out. 'I advise ye all not to be drawn into talk o' Dr Rowan wid her, but not to avoid her personally. Whether we like a patient or not is beside the point. We're here to give a service to mothers and babies, an' Dawn Totman and the child inside her is as important as any o' the others.'

With these parting words, Miss O'Casey left the office to go downstairs to Post-Natal. Almost immediately the telephone rang, and Eve was told that a patient was on her way in, getting strong contractions with her third baby. Thankfully she rose and went to get the newcomer's case-notes from the closely packed ante-natal files. There was nothing like work to banish speculation and brooding over past and present problems. . .and the fact that the maternity department seemed empty without Dr David Rowan's stern presence.

On the Tuesday after Easter Dr Spriggs returned from her long weekend at home. She looked pale, and her manner was distinctly subdued in contrast to her usual vivacity. Several patients had been admitted from Mr Horsfield's ante-natal clinic during the day, and at around nine p.m. the night staff were preparing for a spate of inductions and deliveries.

'I'll assess the three patients who are for induction, Sister,' said Lucinda to Doris Hicks, 'and after that I'll dash over to the mess to see if there's any supper left. I haven't stopped for a bite since midday—it's been pandemonium on Maternity and Gynae.'

'Oh, don't go over to the mess, Doctor dear—I'll make

you a little snack here,' offered Doris. 'There are some eggs in the ward fridge, so how about scrambled eggs on toast? And I've brought the rest of my Easter cake with me, so you can have a slice of that!'

'That's awfully sweet of you, Sister Hicks,' sighed Lucinda, her uncombed hair hanging untidily over the collar of her white coat as she raised a mug of coffee to her lips. Before she could take a sip, however, there was an urgent summons to the delivery room, where Eve was encouraging a large and exhausted lady who had reached stage two of labour but could make no further progress; all her pushes were in vain, and her baby's head stubbornly refused to advance. Lucinda decided to call Mr Andreasson, and at a quarter to eleven the locum registrar had performed a difficult but successful forceps delivery, using the long Kielland's forceps to rotate the baby's head before applying a long, sustained downward pull. The baby weighed almost ten pounds, and a large episiotomy was made to assist the birth of head and shoulders.

Later in the office, as Eve and the two doctors were discussing the relative merits of forceps delivery, Vantouse vacuum extraction and Caesarean section, Mr Andreasson compared his methods with those of Dr Rowan; this led the conversation to the weekend house-party, about which Andreasson expressed some curiosity. Eve asked no questions herself, but listened intently to Lucinda's somewhat reluctant replies.

'How did Mr Horsfield get on with your father, my dear?' asked the registrar.

'Oh, they spent a lot of time in the squash court, and seemed to be enjoying themselves,' she answered briefly.

'And Mrs Horsfield? How did she take to country-house life?'

'She and Mummy hit it off from the word go. They're both into gardening, and talked about perennials and half-hardy annuals all the time,' Lucinda said with a shrug, not looking up from her writing.

Mr Andreasson persisted, 'How did our friend Rowan make out?' Getting no reply, he went on, 'David has certainly got a problem on his hands with this Totman girl, hasn't he? She's not going to disappear, and could make him look pretty silly. He'll have to face up to her one way or another when he comes back from his holiday. Where is he spending this week, Lucy?'

To Eve's surprise the young woman doctor raised haggard eyes to face her senior colleague, and declared in the iciest of Oxford accents, 'I have no intention of discussing Dr Rowan's private concerns with you or anybody else, Mr Andreasson. I just want to finish my work here and then try to get some sleep if I can—OK?'

Mr Andreasson caught Eve's eye and turned down the corners of his mouth as a sign that Lucinda did not seem happy about the weekend or Dawn Totman's revelations. Eve shook her head slightly and turned away. Whatever effect Dawn's remarks might have, she was not inclined to get involved with hospital gossip; it had too often raged around herself.

I suppose Mr Andreasson thinks I'm pleased to see David put into an embarrassing situation, she thought grimly. Little does he suspect how desperately sorry I feel for him, or how helpless to be of any use or comfort.

Well, he'll be back next Monday, she told herself, and we shall resume our smooth working partnership, if nothing more. She was surprised by the strength of her longing to see his face again, and smiled secretly to herself: at least she knew that he was not spending the week with Lucinda!

CHAPTER EIGHT

WHEN Eve returned to Jubilee House the following morning she nearly collided with Andrew Rayner, who was hurtling down the stairs, late for the office. It was their first encounter since the previous Thursday night.

'Whoa, there! Sorry, Eve!' he apologised, having nearly knocked her backwards down the stairs. He put out an arm to steady her.

'You might look where you're going,' she snapped, breathless with the shock of the near-accident. He kept his hand on her shoulder.

'Sorry, my fault. Look, Eve, I'm pleased to see you. I've been kicking myself about the way I—— Is there any chance of us getting together some time just for a drink and a natter? I mean, it's a pity to stop seeing each other altogether just because——'

'Oh, I don't know, Andrew. I'm whacked out this morning after two busy nights,' she frowned.

'Sure, I understand. Are you off tonight?'

'No, not till Thursday, and I'm going to the cinema in Beltonshaw,' she added hastily. She had no wish to resume the 'platonic friendship' with Andrew, and doubted if it was even possible after the unpleasantness between them. Shrugging off his hand, she continued up the stairs.

'OK—see you, Eve, love,' he called as he thudded down the rest of the steps with a hopeful glance back over his shoulder.

She thankfully turned the key in the door and let

herself into the flat. Inside all was quiet, peaceful—and empty. Too tired even to eat, she took a hot bath and crawled under the welcoming duvet.

Eve slept soundly during the April days, grateful for the silence of Jubilee House, around which a profusion of daffodils nodded their yellow blooms. There was none of the hurly-burly of a nurses' home with its comings and goings, voices and footsteps, transistor radios and gurgling water-pipes; no sharing with other girls coming in and unloading their shopping, cooking meals and taking baths; the only sound likely to intrude on Eve's privacy was the telephone, and her acquaintances knew better than to phone during her sleeping hours.

Getting out of bed, showering and applying her immaculate make-up, Eve felt a tiny shiver of loneliness as she looked at the lovely face in the triple mirror. Next birthday she would be twenty-eight—a beautiful, self-confident professional woman with an additional private income which enabled her to enjoy a comfortable lifestyle as well as a very rewarding job: and yet she found herself asking, what else had life to offer her? What had she achieved apart from her position as a senior midwifery sister? Her few love-affairs had all ended disastrously: Paul Mason, Philip Cranstone, David Rowan. Though at the time she had thought herself in love with each of them, she realised now that the only one she had truly loved was David Rowan. He had made a little gesture of friendship towards her before going on his weekend visit to Hallcross Park, but she had rejected that advance because of her pride and jealousy of Lucinda. Now he was in trouble because of a spiteful woman's gossip—and, reflecting on this, Eve definitely made up her mind that she would smile and greet David Rowan as a friend when he returned from his week's holiday. If he loved

Lucinda and eventually married her then so be it; Eve
felt that she could not grudge him happiness. Carefully
putting the finishing touches to her mascara, she nodded
to her reflection and went on duty for her fourth and final
night before a break.

The following day she slept until five o'clock, and then
got up and dressed to go into Beltonshaw to meet Fay
Mitchell at the Outsiders, a popular Beltonshaw wine
bar. Afterwards, at a cinema, they gasped and shuddered
in delicious suspense as the film *Fatal Attraction* unfolded
its cautionary tale, and both gave a cry of horror at the
totally unexpected shock near the end; they joined in the
self-conscious ripple of laughter that swept over the
audience, and after a final cup of coffee Eve drove home
and slept soundly till morning, awakening rested and
refreshed.

It was Friday, market day in Beltonshaw. Eve decided
to go and wander around the stalls there; it was a relic of
the old cattle and corn exchange, and now a popular
rendezvous for local housewives who bought fresh fruit
and vegetables, fish, cheese and bacon at the food stalls.
Good quality clothes and shoes from leading chain stores
were also to be found among its busy aisles, and nurses
from Beltonshaw General were always eager customers.
Eve stocked up with fruit and salad, and bought a pretty
pair of china earrings in a floral design. Depositing her
purchases in the car, she drove to the main shopping
centre, a pedestrian precinct with a large supermarket.

Pushing the shopping trolley along one of the aisles,
Eve turned a corner by a stack of breakfast cereals, and
bumped violently into another trolley coming in the
opposite direction, sending it flying into the pyramid of
cereals. Down tumbled an avalanche of rectangular card-
board packets, and a deep male voice told her to look

where she was going. Her sharp retort died on her lips as she stared into the dark eyes of David Rowan, just about the last person she expected to find pushing a supermarket trolley.

'*You*! I thought you were on holiday!' she exclaimed, outwardly regaining her composure as she stooped down to pick up the cereal packets.

'Here, hand them to me, and I'll soon pile them up again!' he ordered, deftly taking the packets from her and rebuilding the pyramid as if he had been stocking supermarket shelves all his life.

'Considering how well we work together in other circumstances, it shouldn't take us long to perform this operation, Sister West!' He grinned wickedly, and Eve's heart soared as she handed him the last packet, which he placed at the summit of the pyramid with a flourish.

'I thought you were on holiday this week,' she repeated.

'I am, but I need to study for the fellowship, and it seemed as good a time as any,' he replied as they pushed their trolleys to the delicatessen counter.

'How was your weekend at Hallcross Park?' she enquired in a pleasantly friendly manner.

He smiled and shrugged. 'Let's say it was a totally new experience, being a guest at the Hallcross-Spriggses' ancestral home!'

'Tell me about it,' she said conversationally as they stood in a queue at the counter.

'Well, it's a beautiful building, eighteenth-century, probably built with money made from the slave trade, as so many were at that time. Sir Peter's quite a decent old buffer with political views directly opposite to mine, so we kept off that subject. He and Mr Horsfield hit it off very well, and no doubt hatched all sorts of schemes over their brandies and cigars. *Mummy* rather got on my nerves, a fearful snob who started questioning me about my——'

He broke off and looked warily at Eve. 'You'll have heard about a certain lady in Ante-Natal, I suppose?'

'Yes, David, I've met her, and personally I'm not the slightest bit interested in what Dawn Totman has to say about you or anybody else,' she assured him firmly.

'Thank you, Eve. I was an absolute fool, of course, not to make it clear from the start that I wasn't South African. It just didn't seem that important, but—well, it seems that everything comes out in the finish, as they say.' He sighed, but his mouth was hard. 'Anyway, when Her Ladyship started on about my South African origins, I just had to tell her that I was born and brought up in east London. I said that my parents had had a lot of problems with making ends meet in those days back in the fifties—and "Mummy" was distinctly taken aback. Lucy was marvellous, bless her, seeing that *she'd* only found out the day before from the Totman woman, and hadn't even believed her at first. Of course, she was a bit annoyed that I hadn't told her, but she put a good face on it, and said it didn't make any difference to my work.'

'Which it *doesn't*,' agreed Eve. 'Totally irrelevant, I'd say.' She smiled in sheer delight at the surprise that this morning had brought her. Who on earth would have guessed that she'd meet David Rowan in the supermarket, of all places?

'You know, I think I can understand a little of what you must feel, David,' she went on quietly. 'My parents are divorced, and both have remarried. They seem happy enough, the little I see of them. I have one sister, and she's married with four children, and *she* seems happy, too!'

'Ah, so here are *we*, Eve, feeling just a little bit surplus to requirements where families are concerned!' He gave a short laugh. 'It's a funny thing; my being a Londoner seems to be such a big surprise to everybody, but I didn't know anything about you. Hearing what you've just said—forgive me, Eve, but it explains a lot. I just wonder why I never knew before. You never told me.'

'You never asked me!' she teased, and for a moment he stared into her long grey-green eyes that held glints of gold in their depths.

'Next, please! Excuse me, but I said *next*, please!' called out the girl at the counter, and there were impatient murmurings in the gueue behind them.

'Ah, yes—er—a pound of Lancashire cheese and a quarter of coleslaw, please,' said Eve hurriedly. The girl smiled back at her radiant face, and as Eve picked up the two wrapped items her glance fell upon the contents of Rowan's trolley. There seemed to be a lot of food: a whole cooked chicken, a dozen eggs, a large wholemeal loaf and two packets of breakfast cereals, as well as an assortment of tins and jars. She suddenly noticed a pink facecloth and four bars of a well-advertised pink toilet soap. It seem unlikely that these were for himself, and Eve wondered if he was shopping for Lucinda.

'I must get some fruit and salad-stuff,' he said as he put a pound of bacon and a huge wedge of cheese into the trolley.

'Oh, don't get those in here—go to the market, it's much cheaper and fresher,' advised Eve.

'Is it? Thanks, I'll do as you say. I'm not used to doing much shopping,' he said, though Eve felt that his loaded trolley told a different story. Living in his Conway Road flat, he normally took most of his meals in the doctors' mess; of course, he was on holiday this week, but his shopping still seemed enough for at least two. Was Lucinda staying with him at the flat when she wasn't on call? Eve told herself that David's domestic arrangements were none of her business as together they made their way to the checkout tills. Once outside they carried their shopping to the car park, and Eve told him which market stalls gave the best value.

'Before you go, Eve, have you time for coffee? That's quite a decent little place over there, a bit crowded, but it'll do if you'd care to join me.'

Eve's spirits rose again. So what if David and Lucinda were in love? What if he did do her shopping for her? It was his friendship that he was offering Eve now, an unspoken acknowledgement that the hateful past was forgotten and forgiven. She smiled and agreed that coffee would be very nice.

Seated at a tiny table for two, and surrounded by chattering housewives, Eve decided to ask him a direct question.

'When did you last see your folks? I mean at Beck's Cross?' she enquired, stirring her coffee.

There was a very slight pause. 'I've been down to London this week, actually, Eve,' he told her. 'You'll have gathered that I'd rather drifted away from my roots. My father died some years ago, and my mother has married again. My younger brother drifted a bit, but seems to have settled since he married.'

He paused for a moment again, not looking at Eve, and then took a sharp breath and continued, 'Frankly, I was always a bit of a cuckoo in the nest, with different interests and ambitions. It wasn't easy at home, and once I got to medical school I was glad to leave it all behind me. That must sound horribly selfish, but university opened a whole new world for me. As soon as I qualified and started earning I arranged for the bank to send my mother a monthly allowance, and I was able to increase this as time went by, of course. And then I met and married a nurse who came from a diamond-mining family in South Africa, and she wanted to go back home to live. That was how I found myself working in Johannesburg. My contact with Beck's Cross dwindled down to an annual Christmas card and letter, though the monthly cheque still went through, of course, and still does.'

Eve hung upon every word, remembering Dawn Totman's revelations about his upbringing, the notoriety of his family and his embarrassments at school. She could therefore understand his wish to cut his connections with his roots, and also his discovery that this was not possible.

'How long did you stay in South Africa, David?' she asked.

'Nearly six years. It was a great life at first, a completely new start and really quite exciting. There was this professor in Jo'burg who taught me practically all I know about obstetrics and gynaecology. Things began to turn sour when I started doing some work in bush clinics for native women.'

His expression clouded as he remembered and relived the experiences of that time in his life.

'I used to go out to the townships only one day a week at first, but soon I was doing more work in the native quarters than in the modern hospital for whites. My God, Eve, talk about two nations! The contrast was heart-breaking, and I felt split in two, especially as my wife had absolutely no time for my views. We began to realise that there were serious differences between us, and of course her family took her part. . .'

Eve looked lovingly and pityingly at his averted profile as he hesitated and frowned, but she made no comment.

'I realised that we couldn't go on as we were. I couldn't take the political status quo, nor could I change it single-handed, so, to cut a long story short, I saw this piece in the *British Medical Journal* about Derek Horsfield's research into anaemia in pregnancy. I knew he'd be a good man to work under if I wanted to get my fellowship, so I wrote to him. When he offered me this job as registrar at Beltonshaw General on a two-year contract, it was too good a chance to miss, so I took it. My wife didn't want to leave her home, her family and friends, and I can't really blame her for not wanting to give up the good life we had out there. I'd have stayed if we'd had children, but we hadn't, so we were able to get a divorce by mutual consent. I hear that she's married happily now, and I'm glad for her.'

He turned to look straight at Eve, as if to study her reaction.

'And that's how you came to us, then,' she said thoughtfully.

'Yes. I didn't want to stay out there, Eve, but I didn't want to return to the London area. I'd picked up the South African accent, and I've rather deliberately kept it up——' he exaggerated the accent as he spoke, and Eve smiled '——so that you all thought I'd come from there in the first place. I was a bloody fool, of course, as I see all too clearly now.'

Eve wondered if he knew how much more Dawn Totman had been saying while he'd been away. Had Lucinda told him?

As if he read her thoughts, he smiled and confessed, 'Oh, Eve, I do feel sorry about Lucy; she's been so good about the Totman woman. I intended to tell her about my history eventually, of course, but it was a pity that she found out in the way that she did. Her parents felt that she had been deceived, or at least misled, and they turned rather cool. One can never get away from oneself, or shake off ties and responsibilities. Never. And it's a great mistake to try.'

He finished his coffee, and Eve noticed the droop of his mouth and the weariness in his eyes; she longed to reach out and touch the hollow of his cheek, to lay her hand on the dark head and bury her finges in the wavy hair that was showing more and more silvery glints. . .but she knew that she must hide her desires and control her feelings. Any display of emotion would be fatal.

So she just leaned across the little table and placed a cool fingertip on the back of his hand.

'David, you may find that Dawn Totman is going to be more of a nuisance than you realise. Her baby's not due for another five weeks, and she's a real mischief-maker, believe me. I don't want you to give her the satisfaction of seeing you annoyed or embarrassed. . .or upset in any way.'

He looked up sharply. 'Why, has she been talking a lot?'

'Yes, I'm afraid she has. Listen, David, take my advice, keep a low profile, ignore the talk, make up your mind to survive it all. *I* did, and so can you!'

His pale face flushed, and he lowered his eyes from hers.

'Eve—how you must have suffered with all that humiliation, and I never stood by you, never considered what *your* feelings must have been——'

'All over and done with now, and I'm still here, as you can see,' she said, smiling without bitterness. 'And, if there's anything I can do for you to help in any way at all, you've only got to ask.'

'Thank you, Eve, my dear,' he said heavily. 'I'll certainly try to follow your advice, but I hope I won't have to ask you for anything more than that.'

'Just don't forget the offer,' she said as they rose from the table.

They shook hands as they parted, she to return to Mill Green, he to his bachelor pad in Conway Road. Her last words lingered in his ears, and he wondered if he should have told her the whole truth. He decided that he had been right not to burden her with it: he must shoulder his responsibility alone.

Sister Fay Mitchell's cap was slightly askew and her pretty face was flushed as she sat at the office desk and handed over the care of the delivery unit to the night staff. Eve sat coolly listening, not a blonde hair out of place. She was accompanied by student midwife Barbara Gunn and a nursing auxiliary called Sandra, who had not been on night duty before.

'Well, we've delivered them all except for Mrs Joyce Graham, the diabetic mother whose labour was induced this morning,' reported Fay. 'She's plodding on steadily in Stage One Room A. Dr Michael, the medical registrar, has worked out a strict diabetic regime for her. She has two intravenous drips up—insulin in saline, and glucose five per cent.'

'Hourly blood-sugar readings?' enquired Eve.

'Yes—and nothing by mouth at all,' warned Fay.

'What's the dilation of the cervix?'

'Four centimetres when I examined her at eight-fifteen p.m.'

'Then hopefully she should get on and have a normal delivery,' remarked Eve, turning over the pages of Mrs Graham's case-notes. 'It's her second baby, isn't it? Does the paediatrician know that we've got a diabetic patient in labour?'

'Yes, Dr Stalley's on call. Dr Rowan's on for obstetrics, but Dr Michael wants to be present at delivery as well.'

'Quite a crowd! You'll have good practice at conducting a delivery in front of an audience, Nurse Gunn,' smiled Eve. 'Don't worry, I'll be there with you. I'm glad Mr Horsfield decided to induce Mrs Graham. The poor woman has spent so much time in Ante-Natal, and is so nice and co-operative.'

'Yes, not like *one* we could mention,' said Fay, lowering her voice. 'Dawn Totman's been a real menace ever since Dr Rowan came back from his holiday on Monday. She's asked him personal questions in front of everybody, like "'Ow's yer bruvver Sid, Dave? Did 'e ever get a steady job?"—and "Is yer Mum all right wiv ole Wotsisname? We never thought 'e'd actually *marry* 'er!"'

'My God, how absolutely *awful*!' exclaimed Eve indignantly. 'How on earth does he put up with it?'

'That's the extraordinary thing: he keeps so cool about it all,' answered Fay. 'He just smiles back at her and says, "Sid's fine, thank you, and I'm sure he'd send his compliments if he knew you were asking about him"— and "I don't suppose there's any news of my mother that you don't already know." He just doesn't let her get to him. It's amazing, Eve, a side to his character we haven't seen before.'

Eve nodded in satisfaction, pleased to hear that David was following her advice.

'Couldn't Mr Horsfield have her transferred to the University Hospital—or *anywhere*?' she wondered.

Fay shook her head. 'It's very difficult, seeing that she's not actually a *danger* to anybody in a physical sense.

She's a patient—*two* patients, in fact, in need of special-
ised care, and our first concern must be for the health
and safety of herself and her baby.'

'That's what Miss O'Casey says, but doesn't it just
show how few rights *we* have?' retorted Eve. 'Just
suppose that a member of staff victimised a patient in the
same way—what a scandal there'd be and rightly so. The
person would probably be dismissed, and there might
even be a charge of cruelty. So why hasn't Dr Rowan any
defence against this woman's persecution?'

'I must say, it's nice to hear you so concerned on Dr
Rowan's behalf, Eve!' said Fay with a sly little smile.
'They say it's an ill wind that blows nobody any
good——'

'Sure, and aren't ye full o' fancy words tonight, Sister
Mitchell? What wid all these ill winds blowin', maybe ye
should get your writin' done and let Sister West attend
to Mrs Graham—and poor *Mr* Graham, who's sittin'
there beside her lookin' as if he's found an Irish penny in
his change!'

Miss O'Casey was obviously geared for serious business, and the two sisters promptly stopped talking and
got on with their respective tasks.

When Eve had recorded the half-hourly observations
on Joyce Graham, Miss O'Casey summoned all the night
staff into the kitchen.

'Not the office, in case Dr Rowan walks in,' she said,
closing the door firmly. 'This patient Dawn Totman has
been causin' a lot o' trouble, and ye're all to be very
careful what ye say to her. Always be polite, don't give
her any cause for complainin', but don't tell her anythin'
about staff or other patients—do ye get me meanin'?
She's not to help wid the night drinks, Sandra, or any
other ward jobs. And she's not to wander out o' the ante-

natal ward to visit patients in labour. If any of ye run into trouble wid her, come to me at once.'

They nodded, glancing significantly at each other. When Miss O'Casey had dismissed them she detained Eve for a moment.

'And now I shall have to go and talk to the woman about the weather and the flowers o' the spring, just so she can't say she's bein' cold-shouldered, God help us all, Sister West!' She smiled ruefully.

As she turned to leave the kitchen she found Dawn Totman standing at the door.

'Excuse me, but all us girls in Ante-Natal are dead worried about poor ole Joyce. 'Ow much longer is she going to be in this 'orrible pain, do you know?'

'Ah, well now, Mrs Totman, if I could foretell the hour of every dear child's birth I'd be a rich woman by now, and could afford to retire and keep chickens!' smiled the Irishwoman. 'But ye shouldn't be here, my dear, ye must stay in the ante-natal ward or day room, or else this corridor will be like Grand Central Station in the rush hour!'

And, still chattering good-humouredly, she walked along the corridor with Dawn, her arm resting lightly on the woman's shoulder.

Eve regarded their retreating backs.

'Will I ever be as good as Marie O'Casey?' she muttered under her breath.

'Talking to yourself, Sister? A bad sign!'

She turned to find David Rowan looking down at her, an amused gleam in his dark eyes.

'How's Mrs Graham?' he asked.

Eve gave him the details.

'Nice woman, isn't she?' he remarked as they walked to Stage One Room A. 'We must always remember, Eve, that the great majority of our patients are nice, ordinary women and girls who turn to us for help, trusting that we'll do our best for them and their babies. They're the ones that count, aren't they?'

Eve took his meaning, and nodded in firm agreement.

He greeted Joyce Graham and her husband with an encouraging smile.

'Not much longer to go now! Sorry about all these extra precautions we have to take——' He indicated the two intravenous drips and the glycometer for testing the blood-sugar level. 'The paediatrician will examine your baby as soon as it's born, and she might just decide to take it to the Special Care Baby Unit for a little while, to keep a specially close eye on the little chap—or girl.'

'Why should our baby need special care, Doctor?' asked Mr Graham anxiously. 'We've been told that diabetes isn't passed on, and our little boy is perfectly all right.'

'That's true, but sometimes the babies of diabetic mums may be quite large but behave as if they were premature. We like to be absolutely *safe*, and that means being well prepared for anything that may happen. Sister West here will give your wife first-class care, and there's really nothing to worry about.'

Mr Graham sighed, and took hold of his wife's hand as another contraction began. 'Just to have it all over, that's what I want!'

'Look, I'll do another examination now,' said David, 'and then we'll have a better idea of how much longer you'll be.'

He went to the washbasin, rolling up his sleeves, and Eve brought the examination trolley in. At that moment Sandra, the auxiliary, put her head round the door.

'There's an outside call for you, Dr Rowan, in the office. It's a lady, and she sounds a bit upset!'

The giggle in her voice ceased abruptly when she caught the furious look Eve turned upon her.

'Oh, hell,' muttered David Rowan. 'Excuse me a moment, will you?'

He hastily left the room and dashed up the corridor to the office.

'Don't let me ever hear you give such a stupid message again!' muttered Eve to Sandra. 'All you needed to say was that Dr Rowan had an urgent outside call!'

As the subdued Sandra scuttled away Eve turned her angry thoughts towards Lucinda Hallcross-Spriggs, not on call tonight, but apparently occupying Rowan's flat and telephoning him at work—unpardonable! Eve remembered the loaded shopping-trolley, the pink soap and facecloth: what on earth was Lucinda playing at? A few more silly phone calls like that and she would be as embarrassing to David as Dawn Totman, Eve thought contemptuously.

She forced a smile as Rowan strode back to Stage One Room A, his brow shadowed by a worried frown, his jaw tense.

'Look, Eve, I'm terribly sorry about this, but I'll have to dash off for a few minutes. I'll be as quick as I can,' he told her in a low, urgent tone. 'Will you examine Mrs Graham, and let me know how she's progressing when I get back?'

There was a pleading note in his voice. Eve looked up at him, and shook her head very slightly. He knew as well as she did that as obstetric registrar on call he should not leave the building, and if an emergency occurred in his absence the midwives would have no choice but to inform Mr Horsfield by telephone. But there was no withstanding the plea in the dark, heavy-lidded eyes that met hers: he had called her Eve and begged her to aid him.

'Be as quick as you can, and I'll try to avoid letting Miss O'Casey know,' she murmured, lowering her long lashes as she turned away from him and approached Mrs Graham with a reassuring smile.

'Now, Joyce, dear, Dr Rowan has been suddenly called away, so I'm going to examine you instead,' she told her.

'I suppose it's just one emergency after another here, Sister,' said Mr Graham. 'We forget we're not the only ones needing the doctor!'

Eve's heart beat a little faster when her examination revealed that Joyce was in the second stage of labour.

'Splendid, Joyce!' she smiled as she removed her hand and peeled off the latex glove. 'The cervix is fully dilated, so I'll get you moved over to the delivery room. Don't try to push until we get you in there—I'll give you a whiff of gas to ease the pain. Just breathe in and out, my dear, and you'll be fine.'

Summoning Nurse Gunn and Sandra to move Mrs Graham, Eve telephoned the switchboard and asked for Drs Stalley and Michael to be bleeped immediately. As she replaced the phone she found Miss O'Casey at her elbow.

'Where's Dr Rowan?' asked the nursing officer.

'I believe he had a call to go somewhere or other,' replied Eve, dashing to the delivery room.

'It's coming—it's *coming*, Sister; I can't stop myself from pushing!' gasped Joyce as Barbara Gunn hastily washed her hands, dried them on a sterile paper towel and clumsily drew on the rubber gloves, which stuck to her plump fingers.

'Hurry, Nurse Gunn, you won't have time to put on

the sterile gown,' said Eve quietly to the perspiring student midwife. 'Here, look, the baby's head is advancing—place your left hand *here*, and your right one *there*, so; good girl, that's right—oh, wonderful! Excellent! Well done, Joyce! Well done, Barbara! We've got a little girl!'

Mr Graham gave a shaky laugh of sheer relief as the cry of his newly born daughter announced her arrival at five minutes past eleven.

Dr Michael and Dr Stalley both rushed into the delivery room together.

'Well, now, us poor midwives have had to manage on our own, as ye can see!' beamed Miss O'Casey triumphantly. 'Thanks for comin', but it seems your services won't be needed on this occasion!'

There was a tremendous relief behind the bantering tone of her words. Both mother and baby were indeed in good condition, and an ecstatic Mr Graham kissed first his wife, then Barbara, then Eve, then Dr Stalley. Miss O'Casey backed away from his advance upon her.

'That'll do, Mr Graham. Your wife's borne ye a daughter, thanks be to God, but that doesn't mean ye have to kiss every woman in the room. Oh, here comes Dr Rowan if ye fancy kissin' *him*, but I don't think he's shaved since this mornin'!'

A burst of good-humoured laughter followed this warning, and the new baby added a healthy roar of approval.

Eve observed the questioning look on Rowan's face as he realised that Joyce Graham's delivery was safely accomplished. Eve's eyes signalled to him that all had gone well in his absence, and she quickly touched her lips with her forefinger, indicating that the less said about his disappearance, the better. The glance he gave her was full of gratitude and admiration, and she glowed with satisfaction as her perfect lips curved in an answering smile.

But at that moment Sandra the auxiliary called from the doorway, 'Telephone call for you, Dr Rowan!' She glanced nervously towards Eve. Miss O'Casey interposed sternly.

'Your place is here, Dr Rowan. Shall I take a message for ye?'

Her significant look told Rowan and Eve that she knew about his absence from the hospital, that she totally disapproved, and that he would not get away with it a second time.

'I honestly think I'd better speak to her myself——' he began, and Eve noticed that his face had paled. Drs Michael and Stalley exchanged knowing smiles.

'I'll just say that ye're very busy at the moment, Doctor, and will phone back when ye're free,' said Miss O'Casey firmly as she tip-tapped briskly out of the delivery room. David turned to speak to Eve.

'I'm busy at the moment, too,' she told him briefly, without looking up from her task of weighing, measuring and labelling the baby, while Barbara checked the details and wrote them down.

'Eve, I want to tell you something,' he said quietly.

'Your business is no concern of mine, Dr Rowan. Now, if you'll excuse me——'

Because of the others in the room he did not persist, but he gazed for a moment at the back of her lovely neck as she took the baby's temperature. Then, with a smile and a nod towards the new parents, he turned on his heel and left the room.

Eve dressed the baby in a hospital nightie and nappy, and gave her to her mother to cuddle. As she turned to tidy the delivery trolley Miss O'Casey returned and smiled upon the scene. The other two doctors had left.

'All's well that ends well, Sister West,' said the Irish-woman, 'but ye should have told me that he'd gone out, me dear.'

Eve bit her lip. Did nothing escape those sharp eyes?

'God knows he's got enough trouble without makin' more for himself,' went on Miss O'Casey, adding in a softer tone, 'Clashin' loyalties can be very difficult, Sister—like, for instance, I shouldn't be tellin' ye about that phone call I took for him just now. . .'

Eve turned abruptly to look into the bright, teasing eyes.

'I don't *want* to know what the woman said!' she retorted. 'Dr Spriggs must be in a very peculiar state, telephoning Dr Rowan at all hours when he's on duty.'

'Ah, but that's where ye'd be wrong, ye see, Sister West. It wasn't Dr Lucinda Hallcross-Spriggs who phoned him. It was another young woman, and she sounded so worried about somethin' that I hadn't the heart to be sharp wid her, so I just told her that he'd phone her back. And that's what he's gone to do now.'

'But who—who——?' stammered Eve.

'I don't know, Sister, not any more than you do,' replied the Irishwoman as she went over to Joyce Graham and took hold of the baby's rosy hand.

'Sure and isn't she the little beauty?' she crooned.

Eve was totally bewildered. She realised that Miss O'Casey, who normally would never repeat gossip, had deliberately shared this piece of information with her to prevent her from drawing a false conclusion about David's relationship with Lucinda.

She thought about the pink soap. Somehow it had not

seemed to be the sort that Lucinda would use. But, if not Lucinda, then *who*?

For the rest of that night Eve told herself again and again that David Rowan's domestic arrangements were no concern of hers.

CHAPTER NINE

As the April days sped by, the tension in the air of the maternity department continued to increase. All sorts of rumours about Dr Rowan were circulating, and in vain did Miss O'Casey scold any night staff exchanging what she called idle gossip. Eve watched in helpless bewilderment as David's face grew more gaunt, his eyes more deeply shadowed; while Lucinda had quite lost her carefree manner, and was moody and irritable.

One gratifying result of Dawn Totman's revelations was the surge of loyalty shown by the other long-stay ante-natal patients, who told her they were not interested in unkind stories about such a good doctor. She found herself ignored by the mothers-to-be, and was also shamed by the non-appearance of her boyfriend. It became apparent that Dawn had been deserted, and in her anger and resentment she became more spiteful. Eve sensed a crisis looming, and her fears turned out to be justified.

In the early hours of a spring morning Lucinda attempted to perform a Vantouse vacuum extraction under Dr Rowan's supervision, but she found the procedure far more difficult than she had anticipated.

'You need to keep up a controlled, sustained traction,' warned David Rowan, 'and allow the head to rotate as it descends—careful!'

Eve gave a sigh of relief when he edged Lucinda off the surgeon's stool and took over the delivery himself.

Lucinda stood silently by, flushed with vexation as his expert hands brought the baby safely into the world.

Once the mother and baby had been transferred to Post-Natal, Doris Hicks and Nancy chatted as they cleaned the delivery room.

'Poor Dr Spriggs, what a disappointment for her!' sighed Doris. 'She looks so sad these days, though she's stood by David Rowan all through his trouble over Dawn Totman. I just hope he appreciates her loyalty.'

'Oh, Hicky, what a romantic you are!' laughed Nancy. 'Don't say you haven't heard—he's got a live-in girlfriend at his flat in Conway Road!'

'Never!' cried Doris in disbelief. 'How do you know?'

'My dear Hicky, it's common knowledge. My friend, who's an auxiliary on Gynae, saw her sitting beside him in his car—a small, pale girl with big, dark eyes, she said. They were talking together, and he was actually smiling for once!'

'But that doesn't mean they're living together,' objected Doris.

'Oh, yes, they are. He gets these phone calls from her at all hours—Sandra took a couple—he's always very concerned if she calls, and he's even been known to rush home to her!'

'But good heavens, he's supposed to be studying for his fellowship. How on earth can he do that if he's always rushing around for a silly girlfriend?' objected Doris.

'Well, if you really want to know——' Nancy glanced at the door which was slightly ajar, and lowered her voice. 'My friend says this girl's *pregnant*, and he must have booked her for delivery at some other hospital, trying to keep it quiet. . .'

Before Doris could reply, Eve West burst into the delivery room, her eyes blazing with anger.

'Nancy, I'm surprised at you! How dare you repeat such stuff? I'm disgusted by the way these evil rumours get passed around by people who have nothing better to talk about!'

Nancy reddened. 'Time will show,' she muttered with a shrug, while Doris Hicks hurried out of the room to go and put the kettle on. Eve turned off the lights and closed the door. It was just four o'clock.

In the office David was silently writing up the case-notes of the patient he had delivered, while Lucinda sat reading about Vantouse extraction in a textbook on obstetrics.

'Coffee, Doctors?' asked Doris. David shook his head.

'No, thanks, but I wouldn't mind a couple of paracetamol tablets for a headache,' yawned Lucinda.

'Sister West has got the keys,' replied Doris. 'I'll make you a nice malted milk drink, Doctor, and then you can take the tablets with it and get some sleep.'

She went off to find Eve and ask for the drug cupboard keys.

'Strictly speaking, I shouldn't give you anything from the ward stock, Dr Spriggs,' Eve pointed out as she entered the office, unpinning the bunch of keys from inside her uniform pocket. 'However, as we're all here to witness it——'

She checked the two tablets with Doris, who handed them to Lucinda. A sudden rustle in the corridor made them look up to see Dawn Totman standing in the doorway, her purple housecoat clashing with her bottle-blonde hair, her feet bare, and a bold, cunning smile on her face.

'My, oh, my!' she drawled. 'Drug trafficking among the staff, eh? I wonder what the Guv'nor would say—or your Irish boss! When the cat's away, the mice come out to play!'

The sneering Cockney voice grated on Eve's nerves, but she put on a pleasantly professional smile.

'What can I do for you, Mrs Totman?' she asked. 'Can't you sleep?'

'No, I been woken up by the row you lot are making in 'ere. 'Ad a delivery, then?'

'Yes,' replied Eve. 'Now, can we get you a cup of tea or some other drink? Hot chocolate or malted milk?'

Dawn grinned unpleasantly. 'I suppose it's only natural that you doctors and nurses like to 'ave a little talk and a larf togevver. . .'ello, Dave! Didn't see you sitting there be'ind the door. Blimey, you're a one for the girls, aren't yer? Good-looking lady doctor as well as the blonde sister, bofe at the same time! Keep yer busy, do they, Dave?'

Dr Spriggs's nerves, already frayed by tiredness and her failure with the Vantouse extraction, suddenly snapped.

'Sister has asked you what you want, *Miss* Totman, so just cut out the insulting remarks and tell her, will you? A drink of whatever you like, but for God's sake leave off this evil persecution of Dr Rowan!'

'Lucy!' David's voice held both warning and reprimand, but it was too late. Dawn took a step forward and faced them, her pale eyes glittering with defiance.

'I'll give you Miss Totman, Dr 'Igh-and-Mighty Spriggs! You ain't 'eard the 'arf of it! If you're feeling so 'ighly moral towards a poor deserted muvver, let me tell you I ain't the only one! Ask your precious Dave Rowan about 'is little sister! Go on, Dave, tell your girlfriends about poor little Julie, your sister, pregnant and nobody to turn to! Call yourself a doctor—what about *Julie*, Dave?'

'Shut up!' cried Lucinda, covering her face and bursting into tears.

Eve took charge of the situation, exerting her authority as acting night nursing officer.

'All right, Dawn, that's enough; you'll wake the other patients. Come with me to the kitchen, and I'll make you some tea. Nancy, please come with us. Sister Hicks, stay with Dr Spriggs and escort her back to her room when you think she's ready. Dr Rowan——'

'I think I'd better stay until everything's under control, Sister West,' he told her, shutting the office door as Eve and Nancy each took an arm of Dawn Totman and led her to the kitchen. The woman began to sob noisily.

'Quiet, Dawn, quiet now—sit down here and Nancy will put the kettle on. We could all do with a cuppa.'

She put an arm around Dawn's shoulders as a very subdued Nancy plugged in the electric kettle.

'You'll have to get a grip on yourself, Dawn, or Mr Horsfield will have no choice but to transfer you to another hospital to have your baby,' she said gently, thinking of the special psychiatric mother and baby unit at the Withington Hospital.

Dawn sniffed and wiped her eyes, very surprised by the kindness and attention she was receiving from the beautiful and efficient Sister West. She sipped the sweet tea that Nancy handed her, and gradually calmed down.

'I'm sorry, but I just couldn't stand there and listen to 'er sounding orf at me, when all the time 'is own poor sister's expecting and 'asn't got no——'

She was interrupted when the kitchen door opened and David Rowan stood facing her, his face pale and his eyes red with tiredness. He addressed her in a straight-forward manner, and all three women listened in silence.

'You're right about my sister's pregnancy, Dawn, but you're quite wrong in assuming that she's alone and friendless. In fact, *I* am looking after her. She's living with me here in Beltonshaw until she's delivered, and, as she's under Mr Horsfield's care, I'm satisfied that she'll have the very best treatment. I've tried to keep the matter quiet for Julia's sake, but after this we shan't have much privacy. Does that answer your accusation?'

For once Dawn looked shamefaced.

'I didn't mean to say nothing against you,' she muttered, looking down at her teacup.

'Just try to remember that we're here to help you if you'll only co-operate, Dawn. I don't want any more trouble from you, and Mr Horsfield won't allow you to upset other staff and patients. Is that absolutely clear?'

Dawn was silent and downcast.

'Right, I'll leave you in Sister West's capable hands.'

He looked at Eve, and her heart lurched as she saw the pain in his eyes that he could not hide.

'Dr Spriggs has gone to bed, Sister, and if you need anybody up before morning, please call me and not her—OK?'

'Very well, Dr Rowan. Thank you.'

Her eyes conveyed her sympathy and concern, and in spite of the formality of their exchange David and Eve spoke wordless thoughts to each other in that unromantic setting and company: she gave him a radiant smile as he left with a little salute of his raised hand against his temple.

Eve saw at last a way to offer real help and comfort to the man she loved. It would be inconvenient, yes, but she could cope. Her flat in Jubilee House was secluded

enough for an unhappy pregnant girl who needed peace
and privacy. . .

The sound of Eve's alarm clock filled the quiet room,
announcing that it was 'morning' at six-thirty p.m. in the
upside-down world of the night nurse. Eve turned it off,
stretched, got out of bed and drew back the heavy
curtains. The sweet sights and sounds of a late-April
evening greeted her. The tall old trees around Jubilee
House were dressed in their tender new pale-green
foliage, and nesting birds sang in joyful celebration. Pink
and white fruit blossom drifted in nearby gardens, and
children called to each other as they played on the green
after tea. A soft breeze ruffled Eve's hair as she stood at
the window, hugging the secret joy in her heart.

She thought of the scene that had taken place earlier
on this very same day: the bitter taunts of Dawn Totman,
and the dignity of David Rowan's reply in front of the
night staff. Now they knew that the girl hiding in his flat
was his young sister, brought back from London with
him after his visit to his dispersed family and the scenes
of his childhood at Beck's Cross.

Yes, it was a sad enough story, now publicly made
known because of the jealous spite of a woman who had
shared his underprivileged background but not his later
success in life. And yet Eve could feel no sadness, only
relief and thankfulness that Rowan was no deceiver but a
caring brother. So much for rumours and idle gossip!
And by now he would have received the note she had
scribbled on a sheet of headed hospital notepaper just
before she drove home this morning. She had slipped it
into a brown office envelope and put it into the internal
mail for him.

Let him say yes! Let him agree to bring his sister here,

she whispered to the limitless sky across which a white bird flew with outstretched wings. Oh, let him not refuse my help!

Like an instant answer to a heartfelt prayer, the telephone rang. Pulling the embroidered jellaba around her, she picked up the receiver.

'Yes?'

'Eve?'

'Yes, Dr Rowan—David.' She closed her eyes, thankful that she could be heard but not seen.

'I got your note, Eve. I hope I haven't phoned too early and woken you, have I?'

'No, no, I'm up.'

'Good. Look, it's very kind of you, my dear, but out of the question. You don't understand the difficulties.'

'I meant every word of what I wrote, David. I want your sister Julia to come here for the rest of her—her time.'

'It's not that easy, I'm afraid, Eve. Julia's had a wretched life, and has been let down by just about everybody. And she's had no proper ante-natal care, has no idea about a balanced diet or regular hours, and is quite a heavy smoker. Believe me, I *know*!'

Eve remembered how tired and anxious he had looked lately.

'Look, David, will you just give me a chance to *meet* Julia, here at my flat? It would be ideal for her. I have a little spare room, and she'd get exercise and fresh air here in Mill Green, and privacy——'

'But not much privacy for *you*, Eve. You're on full-time night duty, and Julia's not due to deliver for another two months. It wouldn't be fair on you.'

'Listen, I want to meet her, at least. When are you next off call?' Eve persisted.

There was a very slight hesitation before he answered.

'I really shouldn't even consider the idea, Eve. Tomorrow evening——'

'Could you bring her here tomorrow?' she asked quickly.

'I suppose I could manage it,' he said, his voice full of misgiving.

'Good. Bring her over at six, so that we can be introduced and you can both see the flat. It's the whole third floor of Jubilee House at Mill Green, an old Victorian building set well back from the green among trees, between the parish church and the inn.'

'Eve, I——'

'Six o'clock, then. I'll have a meal ready for half-past,' she said with an air of finality.

'Oh, don't go to any trouble for us, my dear——'

'I'll see you both tomorrow, David.'

'I just don't know what to say, Eve.'

'Don't say anything, then! Goodnight, David.'

She replaced the receiver quickly, her heart pounding. The jellaba swirled out around her as she waltzed into the kitchen. Singing to herself, she examined the contents of the fridge and the freezer. She would have to go shopping tomorrow after work, and prepare a simple but tempting and nourishing meal for an expectant mother.

David Rowan was coming here! After the hideous fiasco of two months ago, the cold contempt and the thaw that had so recently set in, he was about to visit her home and dine with her. It seemed just too wonderful to be true. . .and he would be bringing his sister with him, so there would be no embarrassment of being alone together. This act of kindness and friendship would finally erase the memory of that moment when passion

had turned into anger and bitterness. She would persuade
him to accept her confidential help in a crisis, and not
even his attachment to Lucinda could alter that happy
fact.

Julia—or Julie, as she had been called for most of her
eighteen years—was a pale, suspicious-looking girl who
spoke with flat-sounding Cockney vowels that contrasted
oddly with her brother's clipped accent. She was the
youngest and only girl of the Rowan family, born when
David, the eldest, had been fifteen years old. Her nicotine-stained fingers drummed nervously on the arm of
the chair in which she sat in awkward silence while her
brother explained that she was attending Mr Horsfield's
private consulting-rooms in Manchester, and was booked
for delivery at a small Catholic maternity home in
Cheshire, between Beltonshaw and Warrington.

'She's seen Mrs McClennan, the social worker,' he
said, 'and she's making the necessary arrangements for
the adoption. Julia's now thirty-two weeks pregnant,
though she's rather small for her dates, as you can see.'

Eve smiled at the girl, who fidgeted uneasily, pulling
her red cardigan around her. She wore a striped dress
that must have looked quite becoming before her tummy
had begun to bulge. Eve felt a surge of pity for her. She
had met many girls in Julia's situation, but this one was
David Rowan's sister and had his large dark eyes. Eve
welcomed her.

'I think you'll be quite comfortable here, Julia, and
I'm sure we'll get along just fine,' she said easily, handing
them chilled fresh fruit juice from a tray. 'With me being
on night duty, you'll have the place to yourself for quite
a lot of the time, but I'm off three nights every week, so
we'll have plenty of opportunity to get to know each
other.'

Julia glanced towards David and then back to Eve.

'Is it all right if I smoke?' she asked.

'Feel free!' said Eve, who had given up smoking several years previously. 'David, pass Julia the ashtray from the sideboard, will you?'

'But I've been trying my best to warn Julia about the harmful effects of smoking on her baby,' he protested.

'Yes, well, *we* know all about that, but Julia didn't, and we can't expect her to give it up overnight,' replied Eve with a wink at the girl, who thankfully took a packet of cigarettes and a box of matches out of her bag. Eve silently decided that she would encourage Julia to cut down on smoking, using friendly persuasion rather than condemnation.

'I hope you've both got good appetites,' she smiled. 'There's a beef casserole that's been cooking very slowly while I've been sleeping, and it should be just about ready by now.'

'It smells delicious,' said David appreciatively.

And indeed it was, served with crusty bread and followed by fresh fruit salad with ice cream. Julia looked distinctly more relaxed after she had eaten. Eve brought in a tray with coffee and after-dinner chocolate mints.

'Come on, Julia, we'll sit together on the settee, and David can have an armchair,' she said. 'Sugar?'

'Yes, two, please. This is a really smashing place,' said Julia, looking round admiringly at the tasteful comfort of the room, the bright curtains and carpets, the well-displayed pictures and house-plants.

'I had no idea that you had such a beautiful flat, Eve,' echoed David. 'Everything about it is absolutely right, somehow. You've made it very much your own, haven't you? I can't imagine anybody else but you living here.'

'Yes, I've gradually got it decorated and furnished over

four years, and collected the various bits and pieces,'
replied Eve, inwardly thrilled at his admiration of her
home. 'I'll take you on a tour of inspection when you've
had your coffee, and show you Julia's room. It's rather
small, but you'll have the run of the whole flat, of
course.'

The pretty bedroom with its comfortable divan, patch-
work quilt and cushions made Julia exclaim in delight.

'Oh, isn't it *lovely*?' she cried. 'Look at that dressing-
table, David, and my own bedside table with a lamp—
and a little portable telly in the corner!'

'It's very nice indeed,' agreed her brother.

'Oh, I really would like to come here, Eve, it's better
than any room I've ever had!' cried Julia with real feeling.

Eve turned on the television, and the actors in a
popular long-running series appeared on the screen.

'Oooh, I always like to watch this—only David says
it's a load of rubbish,' said Julia delightedly, eager to
catch up with the latest ups and downs of the characters.

'Then why don't you make yourself comfortable on the
bed and watch this episode while I get changed into my
uniform?' suggested Eve.

'My dear Eve, you'll be so tired tonight,' sighed David
as they left his sister propped up on the divan bed.

'I'll be fine,' she assured him lightly. 'I'm off at the
weekend, so how about Julia moving in on Saturday?'

'We'll have to talk business first, Eve. If you really
want to give this plan a trial, we must settle the matter of
payment. I'll arrange for a weekly cheque to be paid into
your bank account.'

'We can discuss that after your sister has moved in,'
said Eve with a certain reluctance.

'No, we'll settle it now, while she's watching that awful
soap opera,' insisted David, guiding her to the settee,

and gently but firmly pulling her down beside him. 'You had better understand once and for all that I'll only agree to accept your kindness on a proper business footing.'

But when he named the weekly amount that he proposed to pay her, Eve protested.

'That's far too much, David, it's quite ridiculous!'

'You can accept it, or Julia doesn't come here,' he declared firmly. 'And, if you change your mind about having her, let me know and I'll take her away at once. Is that quite clear?'

'If you say so,' she answered, deciding privately that under no circumstances whatsoever would she change her mind. She smiled at him.

'Come, come, Dr Rowan, there's no need to look so serious!' she teased. 'We're not in the delivery unit now!'

'No, we're in Sister West's lovely little sanctuary,' he replied with a half-smile, returning her look with an expression she could not quite fathom.

'Yes, you're right, it *is* a place of refuge, and it's the main reason why I've stayed on at Beltonshaw General, in spite of—well, occasions when I've been tempted to leave,' she confessed, lowering her sweeping lashes and turning her face away. He continued to study her profile.

'And now it will become a refuge for my sister as well, Eve. There just don't seem to be any words that I can. . .'

And he stopped speaking as he leaned forward and gently kissed her cheek, a touch as soft as a butterfly's wing. As she felt his lips she trembled slightly. Like him, she had no words. She reached out a hand to him, and he took it and pressed it to his lips, kissing each finger in turn, and then holding her open palm to his mouth. Then his arms encircled her as he drew her head against his chest, so that she could hear his heartbeat. She felt him stroking her hair, and a tremor passed through her body as his strong hand closed over the sweet fullness of her right breast. Still she lay passively against his heart, forcing herself not to return his caresses, though every instinct within her silently cried out her longing for him.

Very reluctantly she stole a look at her wrist-watch, then gently withdrew herself from his arms, lifting up her head and facing him.

'Julia's programme will soon be finished, David—and I must change into uniform.'

'I'm sorry—you're such a temptress as usual, Eve,' he muttered, rising to his feet as she too stood up.

She gave him a level look as she answered, 'Am I? I can assure you, David, that was certainly not my intention. Not this time.'

'My dear Eve, I didn't mean—I've no reason whatever to assume that you——'

'No, David, no reason at all. Excuse me while I get changed, won't you?'

In the privacy of her room she sat on the edge of the bed and covered her face with her trembling hands. How on earth had she managed to keep so still and unresponsive in his arms? Yet how thankful she was that she had! If Rowan thought that her offer to look after his sister was in any way a trap to seduce him again. . .she shuddered at the memory of last February. He had proved that he had forgiven her, and there was no way that she was going to repeat the mistake. She might not have his love, but she was determined to keep his respect now that she had regained it.

And yet he had kissed and embraced her just now, without any invitation on her part. A *temptress* he had called her: was that a compliment? It must mean that he found her desirable, even though he was in love with

Lucinda, and she with him. I must be very careful, Eve decided as she smoothed her hands over her navy uniform dress, and adjusted the neat turned-back collar with its white piping. Seated at the dressing-table, she checked her make-up and reapplied the blue-black mascara she always used. She loosened her hair, brushed it and twisted it expertly into the shining coil she wore on duty, pinning it securely at the back of her head. She kicked off the high-heeled sandals she had been wearing, and thrust her feet into the plain black shoes that she would wear for the next twelve hours. She stared hard at her reflection.

'Take that anxious expression off your face, Eve West,' she ordered, and was satisfied by the cool, approving smile that came back to her.

Emerging from her room, she found that David had just finished washing up, and Julia had done the drying.

'You really had no need to do that!' she told them. 'I'm so sorry that I have to go now. Duty calls!'

They went downstairs together, and met Andrew Rayner in the hall. He gave her a familiar smile, and nodded briefly to her visitors.

'Have a good night, Eve, love. Don't work too hard!'

She saw that David had noticed the brief exchange as she had acknowledged Andrew's greeting with a cool, 'Hi.'

David and his sister got into his white Porsche. He wound down the window.

'What can I say? It's so terribly good of you, my dear.'

'Till Saturday, then!' she smiled. 'I'll look forward to seeing you again, Julia.'

'Me, too!' replied the girl. 'Thanks for everything, Eve!'

She waved to them as he drove away, then got into her

own car and headed for the hospital, her head whirling with mixed emotions. Her common sense warned her that the next two months would not be easy, but she knew that sheer determination would see her through. She would be a friend to Julia Rowan, and earn David's gratitude as well as the substantial weekly cheque he insisted on paying her.

And with that she would be content.

CHAPTER TEN

ALL the maternity staff were relieved when Mr Horsfield announced that he would deliver Dawn Totman's baby by Caesarean section; the ultrasound scan showed that there would be a high risk of haemorrhage if she went into labour, and Mr Horsfield was not a man to take chances.

'She was very co-operative when I prepared her this morning,' said Sister Hicks to the day staff at eight a.m. 'I explained about everything I had to do, and the reason for it, and she accepted it all without a murmur. Actually she's been a lot better since we had that awful scene between her and Dr Rowan,' she added knowingly.

'Oh, you mean when she said all those things about his sister,' said Sister Mitchell. 'You know, Doris, I think she really wanted to *hurt* somebody, especially a man, because she'd realised that her own so-called boyfriend had deserted her. She told the other mums that he was waiting for his divorce, but he's never visisted her. Married men have a way of going back to their wives, and Dawn isn't the first woman to find that out. That's what made her so bitter. The other patients don't find her amusing any more—so they're all solidly behind Dr Rowan.'

Lowering her voice, she went on, 'By the way, has anybody heard any more about his sister?'

'I believe he's found somewhere else for her to stay until she's due,' whispered Doris confidentially. 'She's probably gone to that mother and baby home where she's booked for delivery.'

'Thank goodness!' said Fay. 'The poor man was looking terrible, but now he's all smiles and much easier to work with. The Lady Lucinda's happier, too, not being a girl who hides her feelings!'

'Yes, poor Dr Spriggs has been through it all with him, those nasty rumours and everything,' sighed Doris, picking up her bag. 'Well, I must be getting home to my two tearaways—there's a pile of washing that needs doing before I can get to bed. Eve West's back on duty tonight. Mustn't it be heaven to be able to sleep in that lovely quiet flat of hers? No wonder she always looks so fresh. Mind you, I think I'd find it a bit lonely, wouldn't you?'

'Had a good sleep, Julie?'

Eve set down the breakfast tray on the bedside table. There was a bowl of cornflakes, orange juice, freshly made toast and coffee. Eve drew back the curtains, poured two mugs of coffee, and perched at the end of the bed as Julia stretched and yawned.

'What time is it?' she mumbled.

'It's after nine, and a beautiful day.'

Julia sat up and blinked her eyes against the daylight.

'We're going shopping this morning,' announced Eve brightly. 'You need a couple of nice summery maternity outfits. Come on, eat up—and don't forget your iron and vitamin tablets—I've put them on the tray for you to take with your breakfast. That way it won't be forgotten.'

She had realised during the past three days that Julia responded quite readily to friendly encouragement. There had been little enough of it in her life, and, although she had the ability to learn, she had lacked her brother's energy and determination to rise above her

environment. She had been discouraged by lack of paren-
tal interest and the stress of living in an undisciplined
and unpredictable family.

And, as David had said, she had no sense of time. Two
hours later, when Eve had cleaned the flat and prepared
a quiche and salad for lunch, Julia was still not ready to
go out.

'Come on, Julie, it's nearly eleven!' called Eve. 'We
don't want to leave our shopping too late. I'm back on
duty tonight, and need to have a rest this afternoon.'

As it turned out, Eve got very little rest before the time
came to put on her uniform and return to night duty.
Choosing maternity dresses took longer than expected,
and shopping for extra quantities of food involved discus-
sions about Julia's likes and dislikes. They finally sat
down to lunch at half-past two, and Julia began to open
up to her new friend, telling her something of the Rowan
family background. Eve listened with great interest to
the girl's version of the story she had already heard from
Dawn Totman and from David himself.

'There were three of us kids, and David was the eldest,
the clever one. I remember him playing with me when I
was only small, but I didn't realise then what a tough
time he had, working evenings and weekends on a garage
forecourt while he was studying for his A levels. Our
Mum said she couldn't afford to have him laying around
reading books and not bringing in any money—we were
always short of it!'

From this first-hand account, Eve could picture the
young David Rowan fighting to better himself and escape
from his roots. Some of the stories Julia told about their
father's drunken tempers and early death in a road
accident were truly shocking. Their mother had then
tried to support the family with a series of unskilled jobs,

but she had got into debt and the family's reputation had deteriorated further, especially when another man had moved in with Mrs Rowan.

'Oh, Eve, it was awful,' recalled Julia. 'David went to university, and then my brother Sid left home. As soon as I left school, I got a job as a waitress in a pizza parlour—it was a really nice place, and I got on well with everybody. The customers liked me, and I got a lot of tips. It was run by an Italian, Signor Mantello, who was very strict, but all right as long as you did your job properly. He had a son called Enrico, about three years older than me, and we got on so well together, right from the very first day I was there. He was smashing, Eve, so nice and helpful, and he really seemed to like me. Ever so good-looking he was, too, and—oh, Eve, I loved him so much! He made me happy like I'd never been before. I'd have given him anything, and done anything for him—*anything*, Eve!'

Her dark eyes filled with tears, and Eve put a hand over hers as they sat at the table.

'Then all of a sudden he wasn't there,' continued Julia, wiping her eyes. 'He'd been sent home to Italy by his father, and I was asked to take a week's wages and not go there again. His parents didn't want him to get involved with a girl from a family like ours, you see. It was too dreadful for words. Oh, Eve, why does everybody let you down sooner or later?'

'Your brother hasn't let you down, Julie,' Eve reminded her gently.

'No, David's been very good, considering that I hadn't seen him for years, and had nearly forgotten that I had an elder brother. I couldn't believe my eyes when he turned up again, just after Easter, when I thought that things couldn't possibly get any worse. Oh, I was so thankful! I was staying with Sid and his wife, after a big row with Mum and my stepfather. She was furious when I told her I was six months pregnant, especially when I wouldn't tell her who the father was. I didn't want her making any trouble for Enrico with the Mantellos. Mum said why on earth had I left it so long? Too late to have an operation, she meant.'

'Did you ever consider an abortion?' asked Eve quietly.

'No, *never*! I know I'll have to part with Enrico's baby, but there's no way I'd ever have—oh, I just can't say it!'

Eve put an arm around the girl's shaking shoulders, and looked at her with a new appreciation: there was after all something of her brother in her nature. Eve remembered his scruples about his work in South Africa. Her voice was soft as she spoke her next words.

'Julie, my dear, you're very brave to decide to give up your baby to a childless couple so that it can have a good start in life, with two parents. Please don't let anybody try to change your mind. It won't be easy, love, but there *will* be a future for you one day. You'll meet the right man, and get married and have other children that you can look after properly in a real family. I'll help you all I can, and you know that your brother cares a lot about you.'

'I care about him, too,' replied the girl sadly. 'I don't ever want to lose touch with him again. I know I've been an awful nuisance and embarrassment to him lately, but I shan't bother him any more once I've had the baby and it's been adopted. I'd like to get a job somewhere in the Manchester area—just so long as I can keep in touch with David. . .'

'I'm sure he wants that, too,' said Eve with real conviction.

There was a short silence, and then Julia spoke again.

'What do you think of this Dr Lucinda Thingummy, Eve? She came round to his flat one evening soon after I arrived, and nearly had a duck-fit when she saw me. He told her who I was, and I could see that she wasn't best pleased. "Why didn't you tell me this, David?" she said in that haw-haw voice of hers. "Why do you always try to keep things from me?" She said that he'd never be able to study for his exams with me there, and I know I was a bit of a nuisance at times. I'd get a pain in my tummy or back, and it frightened me, being on my own, so I'd ring him at the hospital to tell him, in case it was something serious. Anyway, she and David had quite an argument about me, and she talked in front of me as if I was deaf and daft. She said why couldn't I go to St Monica's—that's the Catholic home for mothers and babies where I'm going to be delivered. I said I was willing to go and stay there until the baby arrived, but then you offered to have me here, and that saved the situation. It was just at the right time, and I'm ever so grateful, Eve.'

'And you're very welcome, Julie, dear. I must say that you're looking better already.'

'Oh, I feel tons better, Eve. As I was saying about this Dr Lucinda——'

Eve rose from her chair. 'Now, Julie, shall we clear away these dishes, and I'll just go and lie down for a couple of hours? Maybe you should put your feet up, too, after all our walking around the shops this morning.'

'She's keen on David, isn't she? Dr Lucinda, I mean.'

'I really couldn't say, Julie. It's not my business.'

'Nor mine either, I suppose, though I'll tell you one thing, Eve. David's already been married once, even though he was divorced, and he's told me that he's in no hurry to rush into it again, not unless he was really and truly sure that he was doing the right thing. When in doubt, *don't*, he says!'

'That sounds like sense to me,' replied Eve briskly. 'Now let's wash up, and then we'll both have a little nap,' she insisted, not wishing to discuss David's views on matrimony.

When Eve reported for duty on the delivery unit that night she heard that Dawn Totman had been safely delivered of a baby girl by Caesarean section. Mr Horsfield had performed the operation himself, assisted by Dr Spriggs and Sister Pardoe. During a quiet period in the night Eve went downstairs to the post-natal ward to look at the new mother as she lay propped up in bed, an intravenous drip running into her arm.

Dawn opened her eyes and saw Eve standing by the bed. She smiled slightly, and then gave a wince of pain.

'Thanks for all you done for me, Sister. You've been good to me in 'ere.'

'Well done, Dawn. Glad to see you've got a lovely little girl,' whispered Eve.

'I'm sorry for all the trouble I made for Dr Rowan. 'E's a good bloke, really.'

'Sssh. I know. Try to go back to sleep now.'

'You 'ang on to 'im, Sis. My money's on you. . .'

Dawn closed her eyes and sank back into the semi-consciousness induced by a powerful pain-killing drug. Eve gazed down in silent pity at the woman whose jealousy of David had proved to be a blessing in disguise.

Dawn Totman made a good recovery from her operation, and was discharged with her baby nine days later, to face the world as one more unsupported mother, abandoned by the man she had been foolish enough to trust.

CHAPTER ELEVEN

THE bright sunshine of a summer afternoon penetrated the heavy curtains that usually shielded Eve from the light and sounds of day. The bedside clock told her that it was a quarter to three. Desperately she tried to will herself back to sleep, but thoughts of Julia whirled round in her throbbing head. Eve could not ever remember feeling so tired as in the past four weeks, and she had a new appreciation of her colleagues who had family commitments—those with young children to look after, and elderly parents who needed care and attention. There was Doris Hicks, who slaved uncomplainingly for two rather selfish teenagers—and all the nurses and midwives who also had to run homes, do shopping and prepare family meals, wash and iron clothes and household linen, keep houses clean and tidy. . .

Now Eve realised that she too had a commitment: Julia Rowan was dependent upon her, a responsibility that she had taken on and made her own. She had not reckoned on the depth of the relationship which had developed between herself and David's sister.

When she returned home from work in the mornings the girl was always sound asleep. Eve prepared breakfast for them both, and took it into Julia's room at nine, where they would talk for a while before Eve thankfully went to her own bed. Julia quite often went back to sleep for another two or three hours, so the mornings were quiet, but the sound of clattering in the kitchen and Julia's transistor radio would intrude on Eve's sleep at around midday. Even with the sound turned down low, Eve would be conscious of the girl's presence and therefore unable to relax. The sounds of the village life outside would reach her as housewives chatted and children played on the green in the spell of fine weather. Even the scent of roses drifting up to Eve's window was a distraction and a stimulation to wakefulness. She knew that Julia should be getting more fresh air and exercise, but the girl was not much inclined to go out on her own. Meanwhile lack of proper sleep was taking its toll on Eve. She was becoming increasingly tired on duty, which blurred her concentration; this worried her because mental alertness was essential to good judgement in her highly skilled work. She found herself snapping irritably at student midwives and obstetric medical students, and she tended not to join in the office conversations over coffee. Miss O'Casey had been eyeing her shrewdly lately, and colleagues were remarking on her moodiness and haggard looks, which even her impeccable make-up was unable to disguise. Of course there were various speculations as to the reason, and Eve smiled grimly when she remembered overhearing the remark, 'Eve West can't live without a man.' If only her colleagues knew! And how surprised they would be if they could see how calm and patient she always was with Julia Rowan.

After lying awake for almost another hour, Eve decided to give up trying to sleep, and peeped into the living-room, where Julia was watching the television and enjoying her second cigarette of the day.

'Julie, love, will you make me a cup of tea?'

'Oh, right away, Eve!' replied the girl, heaving herself up out of the armchair. 'I didn't wake you up, did I? Sorry!'

'No, it's OK. I've just got a bit of a headache, that's all. I'll take a couple of soluble aspirins,' said Eve, preparing to settle in the other armchair. They watched the programme to the end, and then Eve asked Julia to go out and buy a few items from the little grocery store in Mill Green.

'Take a stroll around the green, and sit outside in this lovely sunshine,' she suggested.

'I don't like walking around like this, Eve—I feel that everybody's looking at my tum,' confessed poor Julia ruefully.

'Nonsense, love! You look really nice in that pretty milkmaid-style dress,' Eve tried to reassure her.

'Yes, it *is* nice, isn't it?' agreed Julia. 'I'll be able to wear it afterwards with a belt, won't I?'

'Yes, a blue one to match the forget-me-nots in the pattern,' smiled Eve. 'Now get along with you, and go out to breathe some good clean air instead of tobacco smoke!'

She spoke with mock sternness, and Julia gave a good-humoured grimace.

'I'm cutting them down, Eve, honestly—only two so far today! And I'm getting quite good at cooking, aren't I?'

It was true. Julia was gradually learning how to prepare the simple, nourishing dishes that they both enjoyed, and this showed in her healthier complexion, bright eyes and glossy dark hair. Eve felt that the process of educating Julia was very rewarding, and worth the sacrifices of her own time and energy—but oh, for a good, long, uninterrupted *sleep*!

'Eve, there's something I've been thinking about,' confessed Julia. 'Do you think that I could possibly have my baby at Beltonshaw General Hospital instead of St

Monica's? I'm getting quite scared of the thought of being in labour, and how I'm going to stand up to the pain and everything. If I knew that you were around, and David, I'd feel so much better. What do you think?'

Eve was not entirely surprised to hear this, but knew that she must choose her words carefully.

'Julie, dear, it isn't for me to say. It's for your brother and Mr Horsfield. You'll have to talk it over with David.'

Inwardly her feelings were mixed. As a hospital mid-wife, she was of the opinion that it would be safer for a first baby to be delivered in a consultant unit, though she knew that St Monica's was a homely and pleasant place with an excellent sister-in-charge. Also, she had grown close to Julia and welcomed the thought of caring for her in labour, especially if the delivery took place during her own night shift; but she was not inclined to encourage the girl to change the arrangements that Dr Rowan had made, and she was only too aware of hospital gossip.

It was past five o'clock when Eve returned to her bed. Julia promised to call her at seven with supper on a tray, but the doorbell rang before the meal was ready. Julia eagerly went to answer it, expecting to see her brother, but it was Andrew Rayner who stood there, asking to speak to Eve. Julia invited him in, and called out to Eve that she had a visitor. He sat down in the living-room while Julia returned to the kitchen.

Eve hastily wrapped the jellaba around her nightdress, and gave her hair a quick brush before emerging from the bedroom.

'Hello—oh, Andrew.'

'Yes, it's only me. Sorry. How are you, Eve? My God, you look whacked out—aren't you well?'

'Yes, I'm fine, thank you. You've met my friend Julia who let you in?'

He glanced in the direction of the kitchen. 'Yes, we've spoken once or twice when we've met around here. How long is she staying?'

'For a while,' replied Eve, not wanting to confide in him. She sat down in the armchair opposite to the one he had taken, leaning her head wearily against the back of it.

'You don't look fit to go to work tonight,' he said, frowning. 'Must you go?'

'Of course I must,' she said impatiently.

'Well, you may say it's not my business, but I care enough to worry about you, Eve. You're going to crack up if you don't get your proper rest, having that girl around here all the time.'

'It's true that I find it tiring, being on night duty and having another person in the flat, after being on my own so long,' admitted Eve, 'but it's only for a limited time, and Julia's no trouble.'

He leaned towards her, lowering his voice.

'I suppose she's a girl who—er—wants to keep things quiet for a bit, is she?'

'That's her business,' replied Eve sharply.

'Maybe so, but it's *you* I'm concerned about,' he insisted.

'Supper's ready!' announced Julia cheerfully as she came into the room with a large tray of soup, ham and cheese salad, bread rolls and fruit.

'Here, let me take that tray,' said Andrew, getting up while Julia arranged three small tables in convenient positions.

'You've met Andrew Rayner from the flat downstairs, Julia,' said Eve, feeling that some sort of introduction was necessary.

'Oh, yes, I've often seen you around—I'm Julia Rowan,' smiled the girl.

'Rowan? Is that the guy I saw on the stairs with you both one evening?' asked Andrew with sudden interest.

'That's right, he's my brother—and he's also an obstetric registrar at Beltonshaw General,' added Julia proudly. 'He works with Eve.'

'I *see*,' said Andrew thoughtfully, recalling Eve's words about 'another man'—a doctor at the hospital. His mouth tightened. Eve was obviously doing this doctor a big favour while he, Andrew, was being left out in the cold.

'How much longer have your got to—er—wait, dear?' he asked Julia, while Eve flushed with annoyance at such impertinence; Julia answered politely, anxious to be pleasant to Eve's friend.

'Another month to go. I'm so lucky to be able to stay with Eve. She's very kind, and my brother and I really appreciate it,' she told him innocently.

'I'm sure you do,' he answered drily. 'Eve will put up with a lot for somebody she cares for.'

Before Eve could think of a crushing rejoinder, the doorbell rang again.

'I'll get it,' said Andrew, getting up and going out into the hall. They heard the door being opened, and David's voice asking for Miss West. Julia rose and hugged her brother as he entered the room, and David then approached Eve, giving her a light kiss of greeting, aware of the other man's eyes upon him.

'Hello, Julia—and Eve, I'm so sorry that I haven't been over since last week. It's been fairly hectic at our place, as you know, Eve, and the fellowship exams are getting uncomfortably close. I hope this isn't an inconvenient time to call,' he apologised, glancing at Andrew.

Eve felt at a distinct disadvantage in her jellaba and with no make-up, but she summoned her natural poise and smiled demurely to hide her inward turmoil.

'Not to worry,' she said pleasantly. 'Er—this is Andrew Rayner, who lives in the flat below.'

The two men nodded to each other without much enthusiasm.

'You'll be able to stay and talk with Julia after I've gone to work,' Eve went on. 'How do you think she looks?'

'Marvellous!' exclaimed Rowan in admiration. 'A completely different girl!'

'It's the way Eve feeds me and keeps me in order,' laughed Julia. 'She's even got me to cut down on my ciggies, David!'

'Then she deserves a medal,' he said fervently. 'Eve, you're a brick. Julia—Julia and I will never to be able to thank you enough.'

He took hold of her hands in both of his, with a look that was reward enough for her lost sleep that day.

Andrew suddenly cut in abruptly.

'That's all very fine, but *I'm* worried about Eve,' he snapped. '*She* looks in need of a damned good rest. Don't you realise that she's now to face nearly twelve hours of night-work? As a friend, I'm most concerned about her, quite frankly.'

Rowan turned to look at Eve keenly, and there was self-reproach in his heavy-lidded dark eyes.

'My dear Eve, I'm so sorry. He's right, you look worn out. I've been selfish and thoughtless——'

Eve rose from her chair with a dismissive wave of her hand. She was furious with Andrew, but had regained her self-possession.

'Please don't say another word,' she ordered, addressing both men. 'I thoroughly enjoy Julia's company. Of course I get tired, like all my colleagues who have family commitments, but there are great compensations. I love

coming home at the end of the night shift, knowing that
Julia will be here.'

She smiled warmly at the young sister of the man she
loved.

'Now I must get dressed and be on my way,' she
continued briskly. 'I think Julia has something she'd like
to discuss with you, David, so tonight will be a good
opportunity. Thanks for looking in, Andrew, though
there's really no need for you to bother.'

As she left the room Andrew muttered, 'I'm going to
keep an eye on that girl, whatever she may say.' He
spoke in a proprietorial tone that made David Rowan
wonder about his relationship with Eve. Of course, she
was free to choose her own friends—and lovers. He
reminded himself that he had no rights over her, only a
deep obligation.

While Eve was dressing, Andrew waited in silence,
reading the evening newspaper and ignoring the Rowans.

'Come on, Julia, let's wash the dishes,' ordered David,
collecting up the plates and mugs on the tray, which he
carried out to the kitchen.

Eve reappeared in her uniform and navy gabardine
with the hood thrown back. Her golden hair was neatly
coiled, and her make-up perfect, as usual. David Rowan
stepped forward and gripped her shoulders.

'I'm sorry you've got to go to work, Eve. I'll take you
and Julia out to dinner one evening as soon as we're both
free. It's time you had some relaxation.'

'That sounds nice,' she said lightly. 'Enjoy your evening with Julia, and I hope you'll consider what she has
to ask you.'

'I'll have your breakfast ready when you come home,
Eve!' promised Julia, hugging her. David also kissed her
cheek.

'Goodnight, Eve, dear,' he whispered, heartily wishing Andrew to Jericho, especially when the bulky neighbour held the door open for Eve and accompanied her down the stairs and out to her car. From the window Rowan saw Andrew take hold of her arm as she got in, and heard his parting words to her.

'Take care, darling! Don't work too hard!'

Rowan's face was a study as he sat down beside his sister on the settee.

'Does that character see much of Eve?' he asked bluntly.

'Not that much, though of course he's always around, seeing that he lives downstairs,' replied Julia. 'Anybody can see that he's crazy about her, but I'm not really sure about how she feels.'

Rowan growled contemptuously.

'Huge great hulk! I'd say he needs to lose at least three stone before he can fancy his chances with Eve.'

Julia looked thoughtfully at his grim profile, and smiled in pleased surprise.

'You're not *jealous*, are you, David?' she suggested hopefully. 'I mean, Eve's so beautiful, and so much nicer than that Dr Lu——'

'All right, that will do, Julia; there's absolutely nothing between us,' he snapped irritably, and then sighed, putting his arm around her and composing his face into a smile.

'So, little sister, what do you want to talk to me about?'

Julia's face had fallen when he'd spoken crossly to her, and she felt timid about making her request.

'Oh, David, don't be angry with me, but Eve said I was to talk it over with you myself because it wasn't her business.'

'Oh, come on, Julia, what's on your mind?' he asked kindly.

'Well, Eve's been so good to me, and she must be a super midwife,' began Julia.

'She certainly is,' he assured her.

'And I'd feel so much safer and happier if she could be around when the baby's born, you see—and you, too, David. Do you think that Mr Horsfield would mind if I booked into Beltonshaw General instead of St Monica's?'

Rowan drew in a long breath and did not answer straight away. He knew that Mr Horsfield would gladly accept Julia for delivery at Beltonshaw General, and had in fact advised it, pointing out the risks to first babies in small isolated maternity units. No, the real question was, would Dr David Rowan mind? The ambitious registrar now studying for membership of the Royal College of Obstetricians and Gynaecologists, as good as engaged to an attractive medical colleague from a prestigious family—how would *he* feel when his sister came in to have an illegitimate child by an unknown father?

Rowan allowed himself a smile as he thought of Dawn Totman and the body-blows she had dealt to his personal pride. The experience had made him a wiser and more compassionate doctor. He nodded to his sister.

'No problem, Julie.'

'You mean I *can* change to your hospital?' she asked eagerly.

'Yes, of course you can. Mr Horsfield will be delighted to have you book with us, and so will I—and Eve, I'm sure. We'll be there with you when the time comes, and you'll be absolutely safe, Julie, you and the baby. Don't worry about a thing.'

'Oh, David, thank you, *thank* you! You're sure you

don't mind—I mean, they'll all know that I'm your sister, won't they?'

'Yes, I suppose they will——' he smiled back at her '—because they'll all see how proud I am of you, that's why!'

Julia hugged her brother so closely that he felt the baby give a kick, and his heart ached for her and the child. Would the new arrival find a good and happy home? How would Julia cope with the parting? David could see no possibility of a happy ending to his sister's situation.

Oh, you poor kids—*both* of you, he thought sadly as she clung to him.

As she drove into work, Eve's tired brain agonised over the embarrassments of the evening. What a disastrous hour it had been! Why on earth had Andrew chosen that particular time to come prying into her private life, ferreting out Julia's relationship to Rowan and acting as if he had a special claim upon herself? Eve felt that she should have dealt better with the situation, but because of her sleeplessness and headache she had thoroughly mismanaged the whole thing. In vain she tried to tell herself that, if Rowan was to become engaged to Lucinda, it hardly mattered what he thought about her and Andrew—but oh, the annoyance of that word 'darling' for the whole of Jubilee House to hear!

Parking her car, she hurried up the stairs of the maternity department to the delivery unit. Sister Pardoe looked up from the paperwork strewn over the office desk.

'Och, is it time for you night owls already?' she exclaimed as Eve appeared at the door with a student midwife and Nancy the auxiliary. 'You've a busy night ahead. We've just delivered a patient who's waiting for Dr Spriggs to come and put in some stitches. You've got two more in labour, and another one's on her way in with ruptured membranes.'

Eve closed her mind to the stresses of private life, and gave all her attention to Sister Pardoe's report. She was thankful that Miss O'Casey was in charge tonight and not herself.

'Good evenin' to ye, Sister West. I'll take the student girl wid me to see to the two in labour, and ye can go wid Dr Spriggs for the stitchin'. We'll worry about the new admission when she arrives!' smiled the bustling little Irishwoman with a sharp sidelong glance at Eve's drawn features. 'And Nancy, ye can start by puttin' the kettle on and makin' a good strong brew for us all. God knows we'll be needin' to keep on our feet, so we shall!'

It was most unlike Miss O'Casey to ask for tea for the staff before starting work, but Eve was grateful for the gesture, which she guessed was for her benefit.

'Come on, Sister West, drink this up before Dr Spriggs arrives,' ordered the nursing officer in the ward kitchen. 'I'll not be askin' ye how ye've slept, your face says it all.'

'It's just a bit of a headache—I'll take a couple of paracetamol,' muttered Eve.

Miss O'Casey closed the kitchen door.

'Now isn't it the oddest thing?' she remarked, her head on one side and her bright eyes narrowing. 'In April it was Dr Rowan who was goin' around like a walkin' corpse, an' yeself as fresh as a daisy—but now at the end o' May he's fine an' dandy, but me best midwife looks worn to a shadow. I'm wonderin' now—could there be a connection somewhere?'

Eve marvelled at her uncanny powers of deduction, and felt almost a sense of relief.

'Yes, you're on the right track, Miss O'Casey,' she admitted.

'She's stayin' wid ye at Mill Green, then?'

'Yes, until she's delivered, some time around the end of June. The fewer people know about it, the better, so you'll keep it to yourself, won't you?' begged Eve.

'Sister West, did ye ever know me to repeat idle gossip?'

'No, never,' Eve apologised.

'The trouble is, me dear, that most secrets creep out o' the back door while we're busy guardin' the front. After what Dawn Totman said, everybody knows that Dr Rowan's got a pregnant unmarried sister, an' she's got to live *somewhere*, God pity her.' Her tone was kind as she added, 'Listen, Eve, I could put ye on holiday for a week in June, an' advance ye a couple o' bank holidays to add on to it, if that would be any help to ye.'

'Thank you very much, Miss O'Casey, I'd appreciate that,' sighed Eve.

When Lucinda Spriggs had finished the stitching she too decided to have a quiet word with Sister West, and beckoned her over to a corner in the delivery room as she removed her sterile gloves and gown.

'Sister West—Eve—I feel that I simply must congratulate you on an absolutely marvellous job. I want to thank you personally for all that you're doing.'

'Oh?' Eve raised her delicately arched eyebrows.

'I mean of course the way you've taken on this tiresome sister of David's. It worries me to see you looking so weary, my dear, though I'm not surprised, knowing what a frightful handful she is. Poor David couldn't get any studying done at all while she was moping around his flat, smoking her head off and phoning him at the most inconvenient times. We're both so tremendously grateful to you, Eve.'

Eve's only response to this well-meant piece of condescension was a disconcerting grey-green stare. There was no way that she was going to discuss Julia with Lucinda.

'Personally I think she could go straight to St Monica's now, and spend the rest of her pregnancy there,' went on Lucinda.

'Frankly, I don't like primigravidae in small maternity units,' observed Eve coolly. 'I'd be happier to see her booked here.'

'*Here?*' echoed Lucinda in horror. 'You can't be serious, Eve! After all David's been through with that ghastly Totman woman, do you expect him to endure even more humiliation?'

'As a matter of fact, Dr Spriggs, I find Julia a very nice girl, and I enjoy her company,' said Eve, turning away to clear the suturing trolley.

'Oh, well, in that case. . . I'm just thankful that she's off David's hands,' shrugged Lucinda, wishing that she had not bothered to thank the ungracious Sister West.

'Telephone call for you, Sister!' called Nancy from the door, and Eve went to the office to take it. She heard Julia's excited voice telling her that she was to be delivered at Beltonshaw General.

'Oh, great!' replied Eve, feeling rather amused.

'Yes, David's been so sweet about it, Eve, and said such kind things to me! I'm so happy about it. Are you pleased too, Eve?' she asked timidly.

'Yes, Julie, dear, of course I am——'

Lucinda came into the office and began to write up the details of the stitching. Eve simply could not resist adding into the phone, 'Goodnight, darling Julie, and thank you for telling me your wonderful news. See you in the morning. Bye!'

She left the office, ignoring Lucinda's questioning look. Let David tell her, she thought.

Three deliveries took place that night, and Eve hardly knew how she got through it; morning came at last, and she drove thankfully home. Julie kept her promise, and had breakfast prepared.

'When you've eaten that, you're to have a hot bath and go straight to bed, Eve,' she said, remembering her brother's insistence the previous evening. 'I'm going to spend the day at David's flat, and do the shopping for him and us, so you won't hear a sound until I wake you with your supper at seven. That's doctor's orders!'

Which Eve was very willing to obey.

Knowing that Julia would be a patient in the familiar delivery unit, Eve felt able now to give the girl real practical preparation for labour. She explained the process of giving birth, and what Julia might expect. She told her about the various procedures that would be carried out—the monitoring of the baby's heartbeat, the internal examinations to find out the dilatation of the cervix and other signs of progress, the different kinds of pain relief—by injection, by epidural anaesthetic and by inhaling 'gas and air', actually a mixture of nitrous oxide and oxygen.

Eve encouraged Julia to hope and plan for a normal delivery, and to co-operate actively with the natural process. At the same time she gently and truthfully warned that nature did not always co-operate with hopes and plans, and this was when modern technology could save lives; by its use the terrible long labours of the past and the resulting tragedies might be avoided.

'You'll get good care at Beltonshaw General, Julia.

Midwives deliver about three-quarters of the total number of babies, but we need doctors for the other quarter—and not just any doctor, but a qualified obstetrician like your brother.'

'Will you still be able to be with me, Eve, if a doctor delivers me?' pleaded Julia.

'I shall certainly try to be around, love. There will be a midwife there anyway. Most of them are very nice, though some are better than others at explaining things. Some are chatty and jokey, others are a bit brisk. You'll meet girls who are only a few years older than yourself, like Nurse Kelsey who's not yet taken her midwifery exams, and others, like Sister Hicks, who are nearly due for retirement. Midwives are only women, you know, and come in all sizes and ages! I'll stay with you if I possibly can, Julie.'

Eve was thankful that Julia's baby was in the right position. Mr Horsfield always performed Caesarean sections for first babies who were in the breech position, with the bottom coming first instead of the head. Everything about Julia's pregnancy seemed to be normal. The baby had grown well, so that she was no longer 'small for dates'. She was not anaemic, her blood-pressure was normal, and her smoking was down to one or two cigarettes per day.

Meanwhile there was another line of action that Eve was secretly pursuing. She paid a visit to the reference department of the public library, consulting the London telephone directory and running her finger down the list of restaurants, cafés and pizza parlours in the Yellow Pages. A letter was written and sent off to a London address, and a telephone call was made. Another letter was written and sent to northern Italy by airmail. Eve waited anxiously for a response, but none was forthcoming. She felt that there was nothing further that she could do, but held on to her hopes and told no one.

The week's holiday, which Eve was able to take in the third week of June, was a great blessing, allowing her to rest and share a blissfully lazy time with Julia. A series of gloriously sunny days came like a gift from heaven, and the two of them spent hours in the secluded garden at the back of Jubilee House where once the children of large bygone families romped and played. A circle of tall trees housed a colony of rooks, whose harsh but poignant voices drifted down in the scented air; the old garden wall was covered with fragrant honeysuckle which had spread along its yellow bricks.

David Rowan, coming round the side of the house in search of them, stopped as he caught sight of Eve lying face downwards on the grass in a white swimsuit, her golden hair loose and flowing over her gleaming shoulders. Nearby Julia lay on a padded sun-lounger, her dark head reclining on a cushion and her pretty milkmaid dress trailing over the side of the chair. Both girls were asleep, and the picture they made was so charming in the afternoon sunlight that David hesitated to disturb them; he simply stood and gazed at them in silence.

Then he saw a frown pass over Julia's face, and she moved her head restlessly on the cushion. He took a step forward, and the sound of crunching gravel woke Eve. She looked up, and rose quickly, her perfect body shown to advantage in the swimsuit, which curved over her full breasts and womanly hips. David stared, and forgot his words of greeting; she returned his gaze, her long grey-green eyes alight with happiness at the sight of him, her lips parting softly in welcome. For a long moment they spoke only with their eyes, unhindered by the conventional words and phrases that so often hid the truth in the heart.

Eve looked upon a man whose suffering had taught him how to be kind and tolerant, and had given him a compassion he had formerly lacked. There was a new warmth in his brooding eyes, a humility that made him accessible even to the most unfortunate and unattractive of his patients, the women who turned to him for his professional skill. He was more willing to try to understand their fears and needs: he was to be trusted, both as a man and a doctor.

David looked upon a woman who had always been beautiful, but now her beauty had a new dimension. She had learned to put the needs of others before her own, and had discovered the joy of real friendship. She had shared her home with Julia, and given up her time, energy, privacy and sleep, without asking for the reward of David's love. She had shown herself capable of patience and endurance, and her lovely features had become softened and sweetened by the hard lessons of the past months.

She was suddenly conscious of her body, and reached for the jellaba, thrown over a garden chair. The spell was broken, and Rowan felt able to speak and move again.

'What a sight to gladden the eye of a traveller!' he chuckled, advancing towards them. Julia opened her eyes and smiled at her brother, but gave a gasp and winced as she started to heave herself slowly out of the lounger.

'Don't get up, love,' he said quickly, bending over to kiss her.

'I'm afraid I must—to go to the loo,' she sighed. 'I can't seem to settle anywhere for very long.'

He helped her to her feet as Eve put on her sandals.

'There's a ground-floor loo that Julia uses, to save her

climbing the stairs,' explained Eve. 'I'll run up to the flat and get some iced drinks. Would you like a sandwich?'

'Can't resist,' he answered as he escorted his sister to the side-door while Eve ascended the iron stairs of the old-fashioned fire escape.

As they sat at tea on the lawn, he suggested an evening drive out into the Cheshire countryside and dinner at the Old Barn restaurant.

'Can't resist,' teased Eve in happy anticipation, and decided to wear her new white Grecian-style crinkle-cotton sundress for the occasion.

'Well, actually I don't really want to go out,' muttered Julia, fidgeting a little in her chair. 'You two go and enjoy yourselves, and I'll stay here. I'll be fine, honestly.' She had scarcely touched the food.

'Oh, we wouldn't go without you, Julia!' declared Eve firmly. 'Is anything the matter, dear? Can't you get comfortable in that chair? Here, let me put this cushion behind your back—lean forward a bit—there, that's better!'

'I'm sorry, but I think I need the loo again,' apologised poor Julia. 'Maybe it's the heat, but I feel sort of peculiar.'

David and Eve exchanged glances as Eve took the girl's arm and supported her as they slowly walked into the house.

David could not help feeling disappointed as he waited for them. It would have been such a perfect way to spend a summer evening in the company of the two women he most. . .

But what was he thinking about? Lucy and he were probably going to get engaged as soon as he'd got his fellowship. She had been so wonderful and supportive

about everything—and was so obviously in love with
him. Everybody knew that. Only. . .

'David! David!'

He heard Eve calling to him from the house, clearly
and calmly but with a note of urgency that made him get
up at once and run in through the side-entrance.

'David, her membranes have ruptured. We'll have to
phone for an ambulance straight away.'

Julia Rowan was in labour.

CHAPTER TWELVE

As THEY waited for the ambulance to arrive, Eve remembered that she had arranged for a representative from a security firm to call at six o'clock that evening, to discuss the fitting of window locks. Reluctantly she scribbled a note to Andrew Rayner, telling him that she had had to go to the hospital with Julia, and asking him to let the man into her flat and take down the details of the estimated cost. She put the note in an envelope, together with a key to her door, and pushed it through Andrew's letter-box.

She put on her uniform to accompany Julia in the ambulance while David followed in his car. It was Mr Horsfield's policy that, when labour began with a sudden gush of the water from around the baby, the mother should come in by ambulance because of the risk of the umbilical cord dropping down through the cervix; the consultant took no chances with this vital lifeline of oxygen to the baby.

As soon as Julia was installed in Stage One Room B, Sister Pardoe did an internal examination.

'The baby's head's still quite high,' she told David Rowan in the office. 'The cervix is only just beginning to efface, and I think we're dealing with an occipito-posterior position.'

David sighed. This meant that his sister's labour would probably be long and tedious, as the baby's head rotated during its descent into the pelvis and through the birth canal.

Mr Horsfield arrived, cool and reassuringly kind to the apprehensive Julia.

'So you've broken your waters, have you, flower? Clever girl!' he smiled, glancing at the monitor beside the bed. 'I see you're getting some contractions now. How do they feel?'

'It's mainly in my back,' replied Julia with a wince, and he nodded, agreeing with Sister Pardoe about the position of the baby's head.

David muttered to Eve, 'The poor kid's obviously in for a long night of it, with a fair possibility of forceps at the end.'

'Oh, come on, think positively!' she chided. 'I'm going to stay with Julia and help her through every contraction. I expect Mr Horsfield will want her to have an epidural when the cervix is about half dilated, and then she'll be able to get a few hours free from pain.'

'But you can't stay up all night, Eve!' he objected.

'Why not? I've done it before,' she answered drily, seating herself in an armchair beside Julia's bed.

When the night staff came on duty Eve was glad to see Miss O'Casey's broad smile as she tip-tapped into the Stage One Room.

'Sure and won't I be glad when all the bigwigs go to their beds and leave us to take care o' Julia!' she murmured to Eve, nodding in the direction of the office, where Mr Horsfield, Dr Rowan and Dr Spriggs were conferring together. Her wish was fulfilled, because Mr Horsfield went home a little later, on the understanding that Miss O'Casey would deliver Julia's baby if all went well, but that she would send for him personally if a doctor was needed. Dr Spriggs came to put up an intravenous drip infusion of glucose and saline solution in routine preparation for an epidural anaesthetic; and

Dr Rowan was not allowed to attend his sister in his professional capacity. Miss O'Casey advised him to go to his room in the doctors' quarters, promising to send for him if Julia asked for him.

Eve settled herself in the armchair with a blanket after drinking the tea which Auxiliary Nurse Sandra had brought in for her. The hours passed, and the warm darkness of a midsummer night enveloped Beltonshaw as most of its inhabitants slept. Miss O'Casey assisted Dr Okoje the anaesthetist when he came to insert the epidural cannula into Julia's spine at half-past twelve, and the girl slept until nearly three, when she awoke with a moan of pain as the epidural effect wore off. Miss O'Casey topped up the local anaesthetic through the cannula; the monitor indicated that the contractions were stronger and closer together, while the baby's heartbeat remained steady and regular.

Dawn paled the June sky, greeted by a chorus of birds in the trees around the hospital and nurses' home. Eve dozed fitfully in the chair.

Five o'clock: Eve's eyes snapped open and she rose at once when Julia stirred and gave a cry.

'Something's happening!' she gasped, drawing up her knees and bracing her shoulders. 'Oh, help me, Eve, please! David! Where's David?'

Eve switched on the light as Miss O'Casey swiftly entered the room. There was no need for an internal examination to confirm that the cervix was now fully dilated. The top of the baby's head, dark and damp, was just visible at the height of each contraction.

'We won't move her into the delivery room, Eve,' decided the Irishwoman. 'I'll deliver her in here, where she's got used to bein', and ye can give me a hand. Call Sandra to bring a delivery trolley and a cot, and we'll do fine together, so we will. Could ye ask Switchboard to bleep Dr Rowan and let him know she's in stage two? He can come over an' sit beside her if he wants, but I'll not have him interferin'!'

She made calm and careful preparations while Eve helped Julia to take deep breaths, hold them and give long, hard pushes to speed the baby on its mysterious journey into the world.

David Rowan arrived, pale but composed, ready to sit with his sister and hold her hand, encouraging her to do as Eve instructed. It was an unfamiliar sensation for him not to be involved as a doctor, but to watch the smooth, unhurried process of a normal birth conducted by experienced midwives who let the mother take an active part in the great adventure.

The door opened, and Sandra put her head round.

'Excuse me, but there's a telephone call for—er—Julia Rowan,' she said, wide-eyed at the scene before her.

'It'll probably be your mother,' whispered Eve to David. 'You managed to get through to your brother last night, didn't you? Do you want to go and speak to her?'

David nodded, got up and left the room while the two midwives and Julia worked together in perfect harmony.

'Another little push, Julia, me dear—good! That's right! And now another—well done! Now, stop pushing, and just pant in and out, like this, so—breathe in and out—good girl!'

And, at ten minutes to six on a bright summer morning, a dark-eyed, dark-haired baby girl emerged into the light, her rosy fists clenched, her tiny mouth open in a piercing cry as Eve wrapped her in the warm towel spread out on the bed to receive her.

'Thanks be to God an' His blessed mother,' murmured

Miss O'Casey under her breath as she clamped the umbilical cord. 'It's a daughter, God love her.'

Rowan came back into the room as Eve was putting the baby into the cot. Without a word, he put his arms around his sister and held her close, her face buried against his shoulder.

'It's a girl, David,' said Eve gently. 'Do you want to see her? She's beautiful.'

He raised his head, brushing the back of his hand across his eyes and quickly wiping his spectacles. His sister continued to cling to him.

'David, let me hold her, just for a moment. Oh, David, what am I going to do? How can I let her go?' Her voice rose in a wail.

'Sssh, ssh, me dear, ye don't have to decide anythin' right now,' soothed the nursing officer. 'Here, just take her an' hold her and know that ye've given birth to her. That's all ye can say for now.'

Julia held out her arms to recive her baby from Eve, and, while she cradled the child and gazed into her dark, long-lashed eyes, Eve asked David if the telephone call had been from his mother.

'No, it was your neighbour, Rayner, asking if the baby had arrived.'

'Oh, *no*!' gasped Eve, shaking her head in disbelief. 'Oh, David, I'm so sorry. It meant that you were out of the room when——'

'It's all right, Eve, it doesn't matter. Perhaps it was just as well. Rayner was burbling on about some message or other for you, so I told him you'd ring him back.'

Eve flushed deeply and bit her lip in vexation. Of all the times to phone! Andrew certainly had a knack of choosing the most inconvenient moments to intrude upon her life.

She gently took the baby from Julia and began the routine neo-natal examination, weighing and measuring the child, taking her temperature and putting pink plastic name bracelets on her right arm and leg.

'I'll never be able to thank you enough, Eve, for all you've done for Julia,' said David, and the slight break in his voice almost brought tears to her eyes. 'I'll sit here with her for a while now,' he went on. 'You go home and get some rest.'

Giving Julia a parting kiss, Eve went to the office to telephone for a taxi to Mill Green. As she put down the receiver, Lucinda Spriggs came in, her white coat thrown hastily over a shirt and trousers.

'Hi, Eve. Is it born?' she asked, her ringing Oxford accent echoing down the corridor. 'David called me just before he left to come over. What's the news?'

Eve's voice sounded flat as she replied. 'A girl at five-fifty. Normal delivery. Three-point-two kilograms—seven pounds, two ounces.'

'Thank heavens for that!' exclaimed Lucinda. 'What a relief to know that it's all over at last!'

'For Julia it's only just beginning,' replied Eve quietly, putting on her navy gabardine.

'Oh, no! You're not saying that she wants to *keep* the child now?' cried Lucinda. 'She'll have to face facts! I must go to David. He needs me.'

Eve shrugged and wearily descended the stairs.

When the taxi brought her to Jubilee House she went straight to Andrew Rayner's flat and rang the doorbell. He answered at once, and invited her in.

'I've got coffee and toast ready here, Eve—and I can soon fry up some bacon and eggs.'

'No, thanks,' she said shortly. 'Look here, Andrew,

why on earth did you phone like that? It couldn't have been more inconvenient!'

'Steady on, Eve, I was only asking how the girl was getting on. And there's something to tell you—I let that guy in to look at your windows last night, and while he was there your phone rang——'

'Who was it?' demanded Eve impatiently.

'I don't know. It was a very peculiar call, and I hope I've done the right thing, Eve, in giving information——'

'What on earth are you talking about?' snapped Eve. 'Who *was* it, for heaven's sake?'

'Some Italian guy. He was jabbering down the phone in one hell of a state, and I could hardly make out what he was saying. Said his name was Morello or Martello or something—Enrico somebody.'

'*Enrico!*' Eve almost shouted. 'Oh, Andrew, tell me, tell me! Was he calling from London?'

'No, it was Savona—that's northern Italy, isn't it? He wanted to know about Juliet, he said, and I asked if he meant Julia Rowan, because, if so, she was in hospital having a baby!'

'Oh, my God,' breathed Eve, closing her eyes. 'Listen, Andrew, did he manage to say anything else at all? Think carefully.'

'Yes, he said, "I fly in next aeroplane from Milano to Manchester." At least, I think that's what he said, he was sobbing down the phone and asking me to forgive him. I say, Eve, is he the—er—father? Eve! Are you all right?'

For she had flung her arms around Andrew's fleshy neck, nearly knocking him over backwards.

'That's the most wonderful news you could give me, Andrew, love,' she cried. 'Thank you! You're a brick, a real brick!'

And, to his astonishment, she kissed him fervently, first on one side of his face, and then on the other.

'It's a little girl,' she whispered, smiling through a blur of tears as she leaned against the broad expanse of his chest.

'Then I wish I got this treatment every time somebody has a little girl!' sighed poor, bewildered Andrew.

CHAPTER THIRTEEN

IT WAS seven o'clock, the time for evening visiting in the post-natal ward. In a sunny four-bedded room Julia Rowan lay propped up against three pillows, her pale, set face framed in a cloud of dark hair. No cot stood beside her bed, as with the other two mothers in the room, happily greeting their menfolk who strode in with their arms full of flowers and soft toys.

When Dr Rowan entered in his white coat he drew the curtains around his sister's bed before sitting down beside her.

'Has the hospital chaplain been to see you, Julie?' he enquired gently.

'Yes, Father Naylor came,' she sighed.

'Was he—was he of any help?'

'He was very nice, but he only told me what I knew already, David, which is that I must put Maria first when making any decisions.'

'Maria? Oh, yes, the baby,' nodded David, his heart aching for the white-faced girl.

'I'm calling her Maria while she's here. When she goes to her new parents I expect they'll call her something else—another name.'

'Have you been to see her?' he asked hesitantly.

'No, not since she was born. If I see her I shan't be able to think straight, David. She's in the nursery, and the staff are giving her bottle-feeds. I'm beginning to get milk, but—oh, David!'

He rose from the chair and was about to put his arms

round her to comfort her as well as he could, when the curtains opened a little way, and Eve's face appeared. She too looked pale, but there was an unexpected brightness in her grey-green eyes, and an excited tremor in her voice.

'Hi, Julie, love! Hello, David. Er—may I borrow David for a few minutes, Julia? We'll be back again soon, and—well, you'd better prepare yourself for a big surprise!'

Julia looked up at her, and could not help feeling a strange thrill of anticipation, even though she had no idea of what Eve meant. David looked questioningly at Eve, who lowered her eyes, avoiding his. He patted Julia's shoulder and followed Eve out into the corridor.

'My dear, what *is* this? Is our mother here?'

'No. David, listen. I've got something to tell you, and it'll be a bit of a shock. You may be very angry with me. If you are, I'm sorry, but at the same time I'm *not* sorry, if you see what I mean,' she said breathlessly, her eyes sparkling with delight.

'No, I *don't* see what you mean, Eve! What are you trying to tell me, love? Out with it, now, this minute!' he ordered, taking hold of her shoulder and looking directly at her, his eyes anxious and searching behind the heavy horn-rimmed frames.

'I've brought a visitor for Julia—and the baby. He has flown over from Milan today, and I met him at Manchester Airport less than an hour ago.'

'I still don't know what you're talking about, Eve. I'm sorry, but you've completely lost me.' After the strains and sleeplessness of the past twenty-four hours, David Rowan felt utterly confused and could only shake his head in non-comprehension.

'David, come with me into the ward office,' she said,

taking his arm and leading him along the corridor. 'There's someone here you must meet, and then you must take him to Julia.'

In the office a handsome, olive-skinned young man stood waiting nervously, his eyes wide with apprehension as the doctor appeared in the doorway. Eve gave him an encouraging smile.

'Enrico, come here. David, this is Enrico Mantello, and he has every right to see Julia—and his daughter.'

David's mouth opened, but no words came to his lips at first. An angry flush spread over his sombre features, and he took a step towards Enrico, who shrank back against the wall.

'My God,' breathed David between clenched teeth. 'My God, Eve! Are you telling me that *this* is the little hero who has caused my sister so much misery—the one who was supposed to love her, but cleared off as soon as——?'

'No, David, it wasn't like that!' cried Eve, putting herself between them. David pushed her aside and advanced on the young man.

'Where have you been all these months? How dare you come here now?'

'Hit me if you like, but you mistake!' retorted Enrico, holding up his head and facing David squarely. 'I did not know she had started a baby! I also suffer, I write letters, many letters—I get no answer, I write more—I get nothing! So, at last I write to my friend Giorgio, and he tell me that my Juliet leave London and travel to north England with another man—she no longer want me. I try to forget her, but no use, I cannot forget. . .'

Eve held his hand as tears came to his eyes, and his words became increasingly incoherent.

'And then at last a letter, word of my Juliet from

Signorina West. I telephone—I speak to man—he tell me—*O, Dio mio!*'

David Rowan braced his shoulders and nodded to himself as if making a decision. With a glance at Eve, he led Enrico quickly out of the office and along the corridor to the four-bedder where Julia lay.

At the same time Eve sped to the nursery, where three cots stood. She took hold of the middle one, wheeling it out and towards the same destination as that of the two men.

David parted the curtains and pushed Enrico forward. Eve had a glimpse of Julia's face when she saw him: he knelt down beside the bed, and held out his hands to her. Julia took them in her own, and cried out one word:

'*Enrico!*'

He did not rise from his knees, and Julia had to lean over to raise his head and clasp him against the soft warmth of her bosom.

'*O, mia Giuglietta, io imploro il tuo perdono!*'

It was a plea from the heart for forgiveness, which was granted in the same moment.

Rowan watched as Eve lifted the sleeping baby from her cot and placed her in Julia's arms. Then she silently drew the curtains close together, leaving the united lovers alone with their child.

Rowan followed her back to the ward office.

'I traced him,' she said simply. 'After what she'd told me, I thought it was worth a try. He didn't know about the baby, you see, and I thought he *should* know, so that he could either take some action about it or not.'

There was a certain triumph in her words.

'Eve, Eve, whatever else have you been up to? This could change everything! He looks like the sort who'll face up to his responsibilities,' said David, shaking his head in amazement, still unable to believe his eyes and ears. 'I'm more than willing to accept him as a brother-in-law if *he's* willing to marry Julia and take care of her and the child.'

'Of course he's willing!' declared Eve. 'He *wants* to marry her! There was no pressure on him to come all this way as soon as he heard that Julia was having his child—quite the reverse; his father tried to keep them apart, and confiscated the letters. But he'll defy his relatives now—there'll be no parting from Julia again. The chances are that the Mantellos will come round when they see the baby, who is *so* much like him—but Julia will come first with Enrico now, David, you'll see!'

'I seem to have done nothing but put myself in your debt, Eve,' said David. 'It's not enough just to say thank you.'

There was a sudden decisive gleam behind the horn-rims.

'It's all right, David, I don't ask for anything more,' she replied, trying to speak lightly, though her heart gave a little bound as she saw the light in his eyes.

'But it's *not* enough, Eve,' he insisted with a note of urgency in his voice. 'There's something else I've got to say. Can we talk now? Is it a convenient time for you?'

'I don't see why not,' she answered breathlessly, her heart pounding as she awaited his next words.

At that moment the ward sister of Post-Natal entered the office, and sat down at the desk to write the day report. She was a plump, motherly Jamaican woman, and smiled pleasantly at them.

'The nursery is vacant, Sister West, if you and Dr Rowan want to talk privately,' she said, and Eve was never certain whether or not she gave a very discreet wink.

In the nursery they were alone except for the sleeping occupants of the other two cots. David closed the door and stood with his back against it.

'What a day it's been, Eve,' he began. 'As if my sister's delivery weren't enough, a prospective husband turns up out of the blue, thanks to you. And I had to make another vital decision today—I had to speak to Lucy Spriggs.'

Eve took a sharp intake of breath. Was she to be the first to hear of his official engagement?

'She came to my flat in Conway Road this afternoon,' he went on. 'Mr Horsfield had sent me off for a few hours' rest.'

He pushed his spectacles up to the bridge of his nose with an uncharacteristically nervous gesture. Eve felt a shiver run down her spine. *Must* he tell her all the details?

'She came to see me, as I said,' he continued. 'I won't tell you all that passed between us—it was all rather difficult and painful for both of us. She's a marvellous girl, Eve, and I'm sure she's got a great future out there somewhere, but you know what she's like, always used to having her own way. She was so generous—she even offered financial support for Julia, so that she could live in a flat and keep the baby. Of course, I could never have allowed her to do that—Lucinda, I mean, whatever our circumstances might have been. . .'

'It won't be necessary now, anyway,' said Eve, unable to think of anything else to say, and wondering what she was about to hear.

'In the end I had to be painfully blunt with the poor girl,' he said with mounting agitation. 'I had to tell her that I was totally unsuitable in every respect for a—I mean, as a —— Oh, dear! And she still wouldn't listen, so at last I had no choice but to tell her——'

He broke off and clasped his hands together as he

looked at her. She returned his anxious gaze in unbearable suspense, her heart now seized by wild hope and fear.

'What did you tell her, David?' she asked, her voice very low, her eyes averted.

'Eve, I had to tell her that there was somebody else. Another woman. That's a fairly unanswerable reason for not getting engaged, isn't it?'

And now the truth was dawning, and not to be denied. Eve stood absolutely still, and managed to speak in the same level tone as before.

'You mean that you are not engaged to Lucinda, David? You're not going to marry her?'

'That's right, Eve. Because I love another woman.'

'And—may I ask if this other woman loves you in return?'

'I don't know.'

And now their eyes met as he asked, '*Do* you, Eve?'

Like Julia when she saw Enrico standing before her, Eve could only say his name and hold out her hands to him.

'David.'

He took her hands in his, kissing the fingers, kissing the palms. Then his arms were around her, and he whispered brokenly in her ear.

'Dearest Eve, I've been such a fool, so blind, so obstinate—and I'll never forgive myself for the way I treated you. Do you know, I'm grateful to Lucinda— and to poor Dawn Totman—and to Julia above all? They've all helped me to see myself and come to terms with my past life, my ridiculous pride. And in their different ways they opened my eyes to see the woman I love—the only woman I love. Oh, Eve, forgive me!'

Her body shook with sobs as she put her arms around

his neck and stroked his dark head, burying her fingers in the thick dark waves, as she had so often dreamed of doing. As she grew calmer she was able to speak and assure him of her love—the love that had sprung so quickly into being, and which had survived such terrible humiliation and rejection.

Gently she removed his spectacles, sliding them into the top pocket of his white coat. The world stood still as they exchanged a long, sweet, deep kiss that said more than a thousand words. A kiss to drown in. . .

The door opened, and a nursing auxiliary stood there, looking straight at them. They drew apart, but not quite quickly enough.

'Oh, excuse me, I've come to take one of these babies out to the ward,' said the nurse in blushing confusion, hastily wheeling out the cot and closing the door.

Eve almost collapsed against his chest as they drew together again in subdued laughter.

'It'll be all over the hospital within an hour,' she giggled. 'Sister West will be at the centre of yet another scandal at Beltonshaw General!'

He held her at arm's length and looked into her flushed face.

'And worse still, Sister, you have lost your reputation as No-Smudge West. I'm afraid there is only one thing to be done in the circumstances.'

He held her close to him again.

'I shall have to marry you to save your good name.'

'Mm, yes,' she agreed, as if considering the matter. 'There just doesn't seem to be any acceptable alternative, does there?'

CHAPTER FOURTEEN

THE last days of Eve's holiday passed in a golden June haze during which she went through the motions of everyday living, visiting Julia each day; she had never seen such a transformation as that of Julia Rowan from a pale and apprehensive pregnant girl into the glowing young mother who held her dark-haired baby to each softly abundant breast in turn, while Enrico sat and worshipped both mother and child.

'I never knew that anything could be so satisfying, Eve,' she said, her eyes radiant with love and pride as Maria sucked deeply. 'What wonderful work you do, bringing babies into the world and seeing so much happiness around you all the time!'

Eve smiled and outwardly agreed with her, though in her heart she knew that midwives did not always witness happy scenes. The Dawn Totmans of this world and the pregnant Julias who had no Enrico to rush to their bedside were sadly unfortunate, and so were the babies born to ignorant and inadequate parents. Eve had also seen the shock and grief of parents whose babies were abnormal in some way, and she had been present at stillbirths, where there was no piercing cry of the newborn, but only a sound of weeping in the silence. Nevertheless she smiled back at the joyful young couple, sharing their happiness in Maria and hugging her own incredible secret—the fact that David Rowan loved her and had asked her to marry him. Every other thought in her head whirled back to the moment in the post-natal ward nursery, and she simply could not believe that it had really happened.

'It can't be true—it can't be true!' she would whisper in the silence of the summer dawn when she awoke. 'It *can't* be true!' she said aloud as she drove to Beltonshaw General on Sunday afternoon with Julia's clean nighties and towels. And yet it *was* true, proved by the answering light in David Rowan's eyes when she met him dashing along the corridor towards the delivery unit.

'Eve, my love, I can't stop—it's absolute pandemonium here right now, but I'll be off call after this weekend. Will you be able to see me tomorrow evening?'

'Of course. Yes, I don't see why not,' she replied with a strange shyness, conscious of the glances of passing day staff who turned to look significantly at them. Heaven knows what they're saying about us here, she thought, but what does it matter if he loves me?

'When are you back on duty?' he asked, taking her hand lightly in his.

'Tuesday night.'

'See you tomorrow, then, Monday. Will six o'clock be all right?'

'Yes.'

'Good.'

And off he strode, leaving her breathless with her love for him, though she had not even spoken his name. He had not actually said where they would meet on Monday at about six, so unless he telephoned her she would assume that he must be intending to come over to Mill Green to collect her and take her to—where? A drive in the Cheshire countryside, with dinner at a restaurant? Or a quiet drink and a talk at the Saracen's Head? What was the difference, as long as they were together, and she could hear the words she so longed for him to say to her again. . .?

Enrico was staying at David's Conway Road flat, and Eve was preparing to receive Julia and the baby temporarily at Jubilee House when they were discharged from hospital on Tuesday morning.

'You'll never get any sleep with a new baby bawling its head off all day, Eve!' protested Andrew Rayner when he heard of this arrangement. 'Frankly I think you've done your share for the Rowans!'

Eve smiled. 'It won't be for very long. Enrico's taking them to London next week to meet his parents. Julia's a different girl now, and copes marvellously with Maria, who's a contented little soul. I'm really looking forward to having them here with me, honestly!'

But Eve was alone on Monday evening when David quietly climbed the iron steps of the fire escape and slipped through the open door soon after five o'clock. He had gone straight from the ante-natal clinic to his room, where he had showered and changed into an open-necked white shirt and light drill trousers, exchanging shoes and socks for leather-thonged sandals.

Eve had put on the elegant jellaba in which she always felt comfortably at east, and was in the kitchen preparing sandwiches to offer him on arrival, with iced fruit juice. She did not hear his approach, but became aware of a broad-shouldered shadow across the doorway. Looking up, she saw the man she loved, his dark eyes upon her, his strong surgeon's hands outstretched to hold her to his heart. She gave a little cry of surprise, and then they were together, their arms around each other in a swaying embrace. She heard his deep chuckle in her ear—'Got you!'—and then his lips were over hers, opening her mouth, claiming, demanding, mastering. Gladly and willingly did she respond.

It had been a long time of waiting in hope and

disappointment. Pride and humiliation on both sides had kept them apart, but now the moment of truth had come, and their meeting was tempestuous. The food was forgotten as he swept her up in his arms and carried her into the fragrant bedroom where she had so often dreamed of him without hope.

She stood passively leaning against him as with slightly trembling fingers he pulled the jellaba over her head, and unhooked the white bra, gently pulling the straps off her shoulders and letting it fall to the floor. Then she was firmly placed on her bed, and knew the sharp pleasure of his eager lips at each breast, drawing up the softness of one into his mouth while his hand covered the other creamy hill and caressed its rosy nipple. She cried out in delicious gasps as he led her just to the edge of pain, stopping short of hurting her; their mutual desire rose up and enveloped them like waves breaking over rocks on a sea-shore. His clothes were discarded, and he removed her white lace-trimmed panties with an urgent hand, sliding them down her thighs and easing them off each foot, kissing her knees and insteps in passing.

'I love you, Eve. I want to marry you just as soon as it can be——'

The words were lost in kisses, and were all that she had dreamed of hearing. Beneath the rose-patterned duvet Eve at last gave herself entirely and without reservation to the man she had never believed could be hers. Never had the quiet hidden-away flat been the scene of such heights of ecstasy, such complete and utter fulfilment as that of the lovers who now surprised themselves and each other with the intensity of their passion.

With all painful memories and misunderstandings at an end, their only delight was to satisfy each other. . .again and yet again. There was no shameful

intrusion upon their privacy, no disappointing anticli-
max, no deception or betrayal of any other person. Their
love was all and everything to them; they were alone
together at the very centre of their world.

David and Eve had planned a quiet ceremony in the
hospital chapel with Father Naylor, the chaplain, offici-
ating, followed by a buffet lunch in the boardroom for
the few relatives and friends they had invited to their
August wedding. They were truly surprised at the
number of medical and nursing colleagues who crowded
in to see Sister Eve West married to *Mr* David Rowan,
Fellow of the Royal College of Obstetricians and Gynaecologists; the news of his examination results added to
the general rejoicing.

Father Naylor ran an approving eye over the packed
chapel, and smiled at the children. David's brother
Sidney and his wife had brought their three youngsters,
and Eve's sister and her husband had come with their
noisy brood of four.

The groom's mother sat beside her son Sidney, a worn-
looking woman with faded prettiness who stared at the
handsome doctor and the proud young mother as if she
could not really believe that they were her son and
daughter. David smiled at her affectionately as he waited
for his bride to appear; seated beside him was his young
brother-in-law and best man, Enrico Mantello. There
were no bridesmaids, but Julia Mantello was an unofficial
matron-of-honour, and the angelic eight-week-old Maria
bestowed her first delicious smiles upon the company,
held up in her Italian grandmother's arms for all to see
and admire.

Sister Pardoe arrived in uniform, straight from her
duties in the delivery unit, and took a seat beside Sister

Fay Mitchell, who was off duty; they were joined by the senior student midwife Pat Kelsey. Behind them sat nursing auxiliaries Nancy and Sandra, and in front of them was Miss O'Casey, who had got up from her bed between nights on duty in order to attend the wedding of her best midwife. Beside her sat Sister Doris Hicks, who stared at the Rowan family.

'That must be his mother and brother,' she whispered. 'There's no sign of any stepfather, is there?'

Miss O'Casey silenced her with a look.

There were rustles as Mr and Mrs Horsfield arrived, followed by paediatrician Dr Philip Cranstone and his fiancée Annette Gardner. The anaesthetists Dr Okoje and Dr Grant slipped in together, and sat at the end of a row.

Student midwife Barbara Gunn came running in breathlessly at the last minute, and found herself a place in the back row, beside a large, glum-looking man on his own. Andrew Rayner had at first decided not to attend, and was wishing that he hadn't, but he felt cheered by the friendly smile of the plump girl who now squeezed in next to him.

A few introductory notes were played on the small organ, and the congregation rose. Miss O'Casey sharply reprimanded Eve's four nieces and nephews, who were fidgeting and giggling.

'Will ye remember that ye're in a place o' worship, and stop your racket?' Dead silence followed, to be broken by sighs of admiration as the bride appeared on her father's arm. Everyone agreed that Eve West had never looked more beautiful, in a calf-length dress of deep cream silk with a rose-patterned border at the hemline and neck; the sleeves were wide and floated softly as she moved. Her corn-coloured hair was swept into a smooth coil on the crown of her head, and pinned in place with a cluster of tiny pink roses matching the small bouquet she carried. She wore no veil, and smiled at all her friends, relatives and soon-to-be-in-laws as she made her way up the short aisle. Julia stepped forward to take the bouquet, and Eve felt closer to her young sister-in-law than she did to her divorced parents and their new partners, though she was very glad to see her sister, and gave her a special smile.

David stood waiting for her, as if transfixed by the vision of this woman about to become his wife. With a loving, teasing expression in her grey-green eyes, Eve let go of her father's arm and dropped a little curtsy to her bridegroom. He made a slight bow in return, and they stood together to face the priest. The mellow August sunshine streamed through the chapel windows as Eve and David made their vows in firm, clear voices that everybody could hear, and all present felt confident that Father Naylor's prayers for a happy marriage and family life would be richly answered.

The hospital catering staff had prepared an unexpectedly lavish cold table in the boardroom, where the radiant couple kissed or shook hands with all their guests; even Mrs Rowan senior felt able to relax and cuddle her baby granddaughter, while Eve's parents and their partners chatted amiably, a civilised quartet.

Enrico felt that his English was not sufficiently fluent to read out the congratulatory telegrams, so Mr Horsfield claimed this privilege, amid laughter and applause. Among the messages was a joint greeting which read, 'All good wishes to you both from Linda Stalley and Lucinda Hallcross-Spriggs.'

'Ah, poor Dr Spriggs!' sighed Doris Hicks, but Eve felt grateful for Lucinda's generosity of spirit.

Barbara Gunn decided that the rather lost-looking man

with a weight problem might be worth holding on to as they heaped their plates with salmon mousse and rice salad, and, after downing a couple of glasses of wine, Andrew felt that he had definitely done the right thing in attending the wedding. He and Barbara exchanged telephone numbers, and she accepted his offer of a lift when the party broke up at around three o'clock.

The honeymoon was to be in Venice, and the flight was booked for the following day. There was much speculation among the guests as to where the wedding night would be spent. The newlyweds were in the process of buying a house in Beltonshaw, and David's bachelor flat in Conway Road was to be their temporary home. Some friends thought that they would disappear into the anonymous grandeur of Manchester's Midland Hotel, while others pictured them snugly installed in a quiet country inn. They smiled at all the questions and conjectures, but would not confirm or deny any of them.

They stayed—of course!—in the third-floor flat of Jubliee House, the place that had been Eve's refuge for so long. It had rejected unwelcome visitors like Andrew Rayner; it had welcomed and sheltered Julia Rowan and her child. Now it opened its door to the newly married couple, enfolding them in its peace and privacy at the start of their new life.

Their bodies were bathed in moonlight as they lay together at the close of their wedding-day. David gave his wife a last kiss.

'Goodnight, my dearest. Sleep well.'

And, encircled in his arms, Eve nestled her head against his shoulder and did as she was told.

4 MEDICAL ROMANCES
AND 2 FREE GIFTS
From Mills & Boon

Capture all the excitement, intrigue and emotion of the busy medical world by accepting four FREE Medical Romances, plus a FREE cuddly teddy and special mystery gift. Then if you choose, go on to enjoy 4 more exciting Medical Romances every month! Send the coupon below at once to:

**MILLS & BOON READER SERVICE, FREEPOST
PO BOX 236, CROYDON, SURREY CR9 9EL.**

NO STAMP REQUIRED

 -

YES! Please rush me my 4 Free Medical Romances and 2 Free Gifts! Please also reserve me a Reader Service Subscription. If I decide to subscribe, I can look forward to receiving 4 Medical Romances every month for just £6.40, delivered direct to my door. Post and packing is free, and there's a free Mills & Boon Newsletter. If I choose not to subscribe I shall write to you within 10 days - I can keep the books and gifts whatever I decide. I can cancel or suspend my subscription at any time. I am over 18.

EP19D

Name (Mr/Mrs/Ms) _____

Address _____

_____

_____ Postcode _____

Signature _____

The right is reserved to refuse an application and change the terms of this offer. Offer expires November 30th 1992. Readers in Southern Africa write to Book Services International Ltd, P.O. Box 41654, Craighall, Transvaal 2024. Other Overseas and Eire, send for details. You may be mailed with other offers from Mills & Boon and other reputable companies as a result of this application. If you would prefer not to share in this opportunity, please tick box. ☐

— MEDICAL ♥ ROMANCE —

The books for enjoyment this month are:

THE SINGAPORE AFFAIR Kathleen Farrell
CAROLINE'S CONQUEST Hazel Fisher
A PLACE OF REFUGE Margaret Holt
THAT SPECIAL JOY Betty Beaty

♥　　♥　　♥　　♥　　♥

Treats in store!

Watch next month for the following absorbing stories:

MORE THAN TIME Caroline Anderson
LOVING QUEST Frances Crowne
CLOSER TO A STRANGER Lilian Darcy
DIAMONDS FROM DR DALY Angela Devine